# The River Series, Book 3: Red River Rising

By Herb Marlow

Writers Exchange E-Publishing

http://www.writers-exchange.com

The clang of the blacksmith's hammer on hot iron sounded way before I actually came in sight of Hank Beard's shop. It was a cool February morning in 1867, but Hank was stripped to the waist and had sweat on his forehead. I pulled Sunny to a halt just at the edge of the shop roof, and Hank stopped banging when he saw me. "In kind of early, aren't you Earl?"

"Yep. We're going after some wild cattle out west of Fort Belknap, and I want you make me half a dozen branding irons. I don't want my riders carrying running irons. Seems to me that's a good way to get hung in the right, or wrong, company."

"Okay, and by the way, are you looking for any hands?"

"You bet I am. You figuring to throw down your hammer?"

"Not on your life! I tried that cowboyin' when I was a youngster, and it was a way too much work for me. No, I just happen to know a couple of young men who're hangin' around town looking for work."

"You vouch for them?" I asked.

"I can for one of them. Moses Alstrom grew up south of here down around Waco. My family's got a farm down there, and his daddy was one of my daddy's field hands before the war. Moses is a good boy, about sixteen or seventeen years old. He's got a friend with him from that same country."

I thought a minute. "That means neither of them has any experience around cattle, doesn't it?"

"Yes, but they can learn. Were you born with cow knowledge?"

I laughed at that. "Of course I was, just like you were born with the knowledge of how to make a horseshoe. Tell you what, Hank. I'm going over to Wilson's store, so how about rounding the boys up and sending them to see me there?"

"I'll do that. When do you want your branding irons?"

"Think you can have them by Saturday? We plan to leave out early Monday morning."

"Sure. I'll have 'em done."

"Fine. I'll pay you now, and pick up the irons when we come in Saturday."

I rode on over to Wilson's store, dismounted and tied the horse to the rack there. I paused for a minute and thought about the first time I'd entered this store when I got home from the war. That was when I'd first met Gloria, at least the grownup version, the prettiest girl in all of Texas as far as I was concerned. That had been a life-changing day for me, and for her. Gloria and I married later that year, and we now had one child and another on the way. I smiled and shook my head in enjoyment at the memories.

Elmer Wilson, my good friend and father-in-law, was standing behind the counter. "Morning, Earl. What brings you into town so early?"

"Had to order some branding irons from Hank. We're heading out Monday to chase wild cattle in Throckmorton County."

"Another cattle drive coming up?"

"Yep, but this time we're going north to Kansas and the railroad that's building there. I figure if we can round up a bunch of wild cattle to add to what we already have, along with the Snaketrack and Rafter G contribution, we'll have enough to make the drive worthwhile."

Elmer rubbed his chin. "When do you figure to make the drive, Earl?"

"The last week of April. Grass should be coming on good by then. Since this is February, we figure to hunt cattle up around Fort Belknap until mid-March, slap the Shamrock trail brand on their sides, buy some more from ranchers around here, and head north."

"Sounds like a lot of work, but then it's goin' to take a lot of work to get Texas back on her feet. Have Spooner come in and give me a list of what he'll need, and I'll have the supplies ready."

"I'll do that. By the way, the branding irons will be done on Saturday, and I thought I'd bring Glory and Ralph in with me to pick them up. Could we borrow a bed that night and go to church with you and Flora Sunday morning?"

"You don't even have to ask. It's been way too long since I've seen my daughter and grandson, so we'll look forward to it."

I'd been very lucky with my in-laws. Elmer and Flora had stepped right in to be nearly as much parents to me as they were to Gloria, since my mother and father were both dead by the time I returned from the war in 1865.

As we were talking about how much Ralph had grown since his grandfather had seen him last, maybe three weeks before, two young men came into the store holding their hats in their hands. "Mr. Lamar?" one of them said.

I looked them over, and they looked pretty shabby, though that wasn't too strange in Texas at this time. "That's me," I responded. "Are you the boys Hank Beard was telling me about?"

"I reckon we are," the young man said. The other boy didn't say anything.

"Names?"

"I'm Britton Shelley, and this here's Moses Alstrom." He indicated the quiet young man standing next to him. Alstrom nodded.

"I understand you two are lookin' for work. Ever been around longhorn cattle?"

"Not a lot, Mr. Lamar, but we're fast learners," Shelley replied, and Alstrom looked hopeful.

I smiled at that sally. "Well, boys, I'll give you a tryout. I'm fixin' to take a crew out to Throckmorton County to gather wild cattle for a drive north later on. If you want to work, I'll pay you twenty dollars a month and found."

They both beamed. "Thank you, Mr. Lamar," Shelley said. "We'll work real hard."

I laughed. "Son, you don't have any idea how hard you're going to work. You'll earn every penny of your wages, and then some. Now, do you have horses?"

They hung their heads, I guess thinking if that was a condition of the job they were unemployed again. "No, sir."

"Well, don't worry about it. Be here at the store Sunday afternoon and you can go back to the ranch with my family. Got any money?"

Again, "No, sir."

I dug out a ten dollar gold piece and gave it to Shelley. "This will give you $5.00 a piece, and I'll deduct it from your first paychecks."

Their faces lighted up. "Thank you, sir!" Shelley said.

They put their hats on and started to leave, but I stopped them. "It doesn't really make much difference, but I'd like to know if Moses can talk."

He gave me a brilliant smile, his teeth bright white against his dusky skin. "Yes, sir, I can."

We all laughed, and the boys went through the door. Elmer shook his head. "Looks to me like you've got your work cut out making cowboys out of those two."

"Probably so, Elmer, but everybody has to start somewhere."

"How'd your horse hunt turn out, Earl? I know you and Pablo went out to West Texas a few weeks ago chasing broomtails."

"Went well, Elmer. I felt kind of like those two boys that were just here, though. Those friends of Pablo's never made a wrong move, and of course Pablo is the best horseman in several counties. Still, I tried to hold my own. We came back with sixteen head of good horseflesh, and Pablo's got most of them ready to go by now."

Pablo Esperanza had come to the ranch looking for work, and Lady Luck had really smiled on us. Pablo had a way with horses that had to be seen to be believed. When I hired him, he brought his wife, Juanita, and baby boy, Ramon with him. They now made up part of the L Bar family, and Pablo made sure we had the best mounts in the county.

It was late afternoon when I got back to the L Bar. I paused on the rise as I usually did where I could look down on the buildings and feel the pride of knowing this was my home, the place where my children would grow strong, and where Gloria and I could grow old together.

My mother and father had built the ranch together, and while I still missed them, I knew they were smiling down on the place now. My one regret was that they never lived to know their daughter-in-law and see their grandchild.

When I stopped my horse at the barn, Hutch came out to meet me. "Didn't happen to hire any hands in town, did you?"

I grinned at him. "Well, Mister Foreman, I did and I didn't. Hank Beard recommended a couple of farm boys, so I put them on for the drive. They'll be coming back with us on Sunday."

Hutch didn't match my grin. He was a good foreman, and right now he was all business. "Earl, you've got a soft heart, but we need hands, not boys. I figure if we had a couple more men who could swing a rope, we'd be a lot better off."

"You're right about that, but we'd probably have to go all the way to Fort Worth to find any, and we just don't have the time."

"Alright, but those boys could be more trouble than they're worth?"

"Could be, but I don't think so. Besides, the farm boys can wrangle and help Spooner, and that'll release Davido to work with Pablo, and that boy's turning into a real hand with a rope."

Hutch didn't really agree, but he couldn't think of anything better, so we left it at that. He headed for the hay barn, and I went up to the house. Hutch was a good foreman, trained by my dad. He was not only a good cowman, but he knew how to work the hands without resentment. Some ranchers that I knew had a steady turnover of cowboys--or at least they had before the war--but our hands never seemed to want to leave, and that was fine with me.

My pa had constructed all of the buildings on the place, or had them constructed under his supervision, and he had been especially particular about the house. Ma was a girl far from her home down by San Antonio, and to make up for taking her so far away, her new husband built her the finest house in the country. Folks used to come from all over just to see the bathroom in the house with a built in tub.

I stepped up on the long front porch and had my hand on the latch when the door opened. There stood Gloria, and she was a sight that I never tired of seeing. This was the young woman that had come bursting into my life as soon as I returned from the war. In a flash the memory of our first meeting came into my mind. Today, she had her shining dark hair down as she had on that day, and her eyes snapped with love and life. Glory was as pretty as a full moon.

"Earl, it's so good to have you home," she said as she rushed into my arms, as if I'd been gone for a week. I hugged her, but not too tight, for she was in her sixth month of pregnancy.

"Babe, you'll never know how much I look forward to coming home to you."

She laughed and replied, "I'll bet I do!"

We went on into the house, and Rachel came in from the kitchen carrying our son Ralph. The minute he saw me, he cried, "Da!" and wriggled to get down. She sat him on the floor and he started to walk toward me, but walking was way too slow. Down he went onto his hands and knees and raced across the floor. I caught him up and tossed him over my head, and he laughed as only a baby can. Ralph was nine months old and as healthy as a little boy could be.

Later, at the supper table, I looked at the families gathered there: Jimbo and Rachel with their little boy David now three years old, and Pablo, Juanita and little Ramon about the same age. With me and Glory and little Ralph, we filled the kitchen pretty well. "Family," I said, "Gloria and I are going into town on Saturday and stay over with her folks that night. Sunday afternoon we'll come back home, and we'll bring a couple of farm boys I hired today to make the gather in Throckmorton County. Monday morning early we'll head out, and I figure we'll be gone for about two weeks.

"Now, you ladies will be staying here, and we don't really have a man to stay with you, since we're going to need all the help we can get. Will that be all right with you? If not, say so, and we'll try to make other arrangements."

They talked it back and forth, but the upshot was that they agreed they'd rather stay by themselves so we could finish the gather and get back home sooner. Juanita, the quietest of the three, sort of summed it up. "Senor Earl," she and Pablo clung to the Senor in front of my name, though I had asked them many times to just call me Earl without the title. In the same way, both Jimbo and Rachel called me Mister Earl. "We will be fine, and when you come home we will have a big dinner to welcome you."

I smiled at her, and Jimbo said, "Now, with that to look forward to, you can bet we'll be back here as soon as possible." Pablo and I voiced our agreement.

Gloria wasn't the only woman on the L Bar that was expecting another child. Though nobody mentioned it, both of the other women were fixing to increase our population, too. I didn't really like leaving them alone while we were gone, but they were right in one thing: the more men we had with us, the quicker we'd gather the cattle and get back home.

I had asked our neighbor to the west, Sean O'Sullivan to look in from time to time, and he agreed. Sean on the west, and Hattie Groves, bordering the L Bar on the east, had thrown cattle into a joint herd for our first two drives, and this time they were planning to do the same, and they working their own places while we were gone.

It was nearing noontime when we got to the Wilson's in Meridian on Saturday. Flora was expecting us, and the table was groaning with her good food. We had left a busy crew on the ranch as final preparations were being made for the drive, and none of the hands had come in with us.

After eating Flora's fine cooking, I drove the buggy down to the blacksmith's shop and picked up the new branding irons. Hank told me the boys that I'd hired had told him about meeting us the next day. "That ten dollars you gave them was burning a hole in their pockets, but they listened when I told them to make it last. I happened to have ten silver dollars, so I made change for them, and they each left two of the dollars with me. Who knows what they spent the rest on."

"I reckon we'll see. Where are they staying?"

"Well, my house is small, so we don't have room for two big-footed boys, but we've got a wood shed that fits them pretty good."

Laughing at Hank the lost-boy-hotel-keeper, I left the team and buggy at his hitch rail and walked on over to the jail to say hello to the sheriff. "Stan," I said, shaking his hand, "anything new with you?"

"Not much, Earl, although it looks like some changes are coming for Texas. I've got a week old newspaper from Austin that says the reconstruction idea of President Johnson will be set aside by the congress. We may have a Yankee general runnin' things here in Texas."

"You mean, the governor will have to take orders from the Yankee military?"

"Kind of looks like it."

"Well, I'm not surprised. I know when my cavalry unit was disbanded in Louisiana, a Yankee officer told us we'd be watched pretty close to make sure we didn't try to rebel again. I figured at the time that there'd be Union soldiers all over the state. Doesn't matter much to me right now, though. I've got wild cattle on my mind."

"Good luck with your roundup."

Chapter Three

The rest of the day was a peaceful one for Glory and me. Elmer kept the store open, and being Saturday there were quite a few customers, many of them I knew and it was good to see old friends. We visited about various things, and after he closed the store, Elmer opened his safe, and my bank, so I could take some money out for the expenses I knew would be coming up.

There was a bank in town, though it was closed now. The former banker, a Yankee named Emeril Goethe--nicknamed Banker Goat by the townspeople, a play on the German pronunciation of his last name--had it open for a while the year before, but he'd been caught for kidnapping the L Bar women, and Elmer and Flora Wilson, my in-laws. Right now he and several of his outlaws were residing in the Fort Worth jail awaiting trial.

When I returned from a cattle drive on the Goodnight-Loving Trail the summer before, Elmer had allowed me to put sixty-five hundred dollars in gold in his large, well-hidden safe. I had drawn on that money for ranch supplies, payroll and fixings, but there was still nearly five thousand left. I took $300.00 out, placing the coins in a money belt I'd brought for that purpose.

"Thanks for being the bank, Elmer."

"Not a problem," he replied, closing the safe behind the panel that hid it. "Do you know there's a dance at the schoolhouse tonight?"

"No, I don't, but Glory probably does. Afraid though, in her condition, dancing's not on the program."

He grinned at me. "Probably not, though I'll bet she'll want to go. By the way, when is she due?"

"In June sometime." Elmer gave me look with his eyebrows arched. "I know, I know," I said, feeling guilty, "and yes I'll probably be gone again, but there's not much I can do about that now."

He laughed at me. "Poor planning, Mr. Lamar. Very poor planning." I acted like I was going to hit him, and he ducked.

Sure enough, at supper Gloria and Flora announced that they wanted to go to the dance. Elmer and I halfheartedly tried to talk them out of it, but we knew we were pushing a lost cause. The upshot was that we all went to the dance, including little Ralph. At one end of the large schoolroom, tables had been set up and they were groaning with food. Gloria and Flora made a beeline for the group of matrons and children gathered there to leave their own offerings and catch up on the latest gossip, and Elmer and I stepped back outside to visit with the men gathered around a large fire.

The talk was all about the change in the Yankee occupation, and wondering what would happen to Texas now. One man, a big rough looking fellow with lank black hair and tobacco juice tracks down the corners of his mouth, had a lot to say about how we should just rebel again and run all the Yankees out of the state.

When I could, I pulled Stan Baldwin aside and asked, "Who is that loudmouth?"

"Name's Justus Dearborn. Didn't go to the army because he claims to have a bad back. The story behind that is that he hid out from the conscription officers when they came around in the last year of the war. Anyway, he always has something to say about everything."

"Well, if he's getting' up another rebel army, I'll pass." The sheriff chuckled and agreed that he would too.

We rejoined the group, but I soon tired of the talk and went back into the building. For music, there was a fiddler and a guitar picker, and while they were tuning up, I passed them by and went to see how Gloria was doing. She smiled up at me, and I took little Ralph from her. "You know, Earl, I haven't danced with you since our engagement party."

"Well, Mrs. Lamar, I reckon we ought to correct that," I replied, handing Ralph to his grandmother.

The music was starting, and it was slow, so I took hold of her and we moved out onto the floor. I wasn't really much of a dancer, but with Gloria in my arms, every step seemed to be the right one.

I whispered in her ear, "You're as light as a feather, babe, and if you weren't already my wife, I'd be courting you in a heartbeat."

Glory gave me her sweetest smile, and once again I saw in my mind that pretty face in Wilson's Store that I'd fell for like a ton of bricks when I first came back from the war. If I lived to be ninety I'd never tire of looking at her.

I heard a ruckus and turned to see Justus Dearborn shoving his way through a crowd of hopefuls, mouth going and spewing words. One of the young men in the group grabbed Dearborn by the arm to stop his headlong rush, but the bigger man pulled his arm loose and turned to take a swipe at the smaller one. The dancing stopped, and once I made sure the women and kids were all behind the tables, I moved toward the noise.

Dearborn had landed a blow on the young man's chest, and he pulled his arm back to hit him again, but I grabbed his right arm and shoved it up behind him, twisting my left hand in the dirty collar of his shirt. He gave a shout of pain and tried to get free, but I simply pushed up harder and turned him around to aim for the door. Just as I got him there, Sheriff Baldwin came up the steps. "Sheriff," I said, "You might want to put this bag of wind in a jail cell to cool off. He was trying to pick a fight with a man about half his size."

Justus Dearborn was yelling that I was breaking his arm and wanting me arrested, but Stan just grinned at him. "Well, Earl, since you've got such a good hold on him, why don't you just march him on over to the jail and I'll lock him up."

And that's what we did. Once the man was in a cell, he was still braying, but by the time Stan and I got back into his office closing two doors behind us, all we could hear was muffled irritating noise. We grinned at each other and headed back to the dance.

After church the next day, and another of Flora's fine meals, we set out for home in a misty rain, with two quiet young men sitting in back. Now rain in

Bosque County happened seldom enough to always be welcome, and the smell of wet ground made the trip home a pleasant one, and the top on the carriage keeping us mostly dry. Once we crossed the Bosque River, Glory said, "Just how long do you think you'll be gone in Throckmorton County, Earl?"

"Probably no more than two weeks, babe. We're not going to comb the country dry, just round up as many mavericks as we can. From what Hutch learned from his friend west of Fort Belknap, there are a lot of wild cattle out there in the draws and brush along the Brazos."

"And when you get back you're going to take off immediately for the Red River?"

"Well, it will be a couple more weeks. We want to gather our own cattle, and work the ones we get in Throckmorton County, so that'll take a while.

"The trail boss I talked too last fall when we were in Fort Worth told me that he was heading for Baxter Springs, Kansas, right down in the southeast corner of that state where the railroad ends. He called it the 'Shawnee Trail', and it goes through Indian Territory."

"I'm not very good at geography, Earl, but that seems like a long ways away," she said kind of sadly.

"It is, but not a lot further than the trip I made to New Mexico with Colonel Goodnight, and there's a lot more water along the way."

The year before I had promised to take Gloria with me on the next cattle drive, but we both knew that with little Ralph in her arms, and another baby on the way, that was not possible. I reached over and held her hand for a bit, and she leaned her head on my shoulder. Neither of us said so, but we both knew that no matter how long I'd be gone, it would be *too* long.

When we got home, the boys and I put the team up while Glory took a very sleepy baby to the house for a nap. Hutch came to meet his new cowhands, and I made the introductions. "Come on with me, boys," Hutch said, "and I'll introduce you to the rest of the crew."

Like all young green hands, Britt and Moses were in for some hazing and hoorawing from the older men, but that was part of growing up in cattle country. I remembered the tricks Red and Bill had pulled on me what I was a youngster, and while I'd not want to go through that again, it was part of making me the man I now was.

Supper that night was kind of subdued until I said, "Now, if you girls want your men to be all sad and woebegone while they're gone, you're sure goin' at it the right way; I haven't seen so many frowns since General Lee surrendered. Jimbo, lead us in a song, and not one of your sad songs, either."

Jimbo gave me a slow smile and began to sing "Sweet Betsy From Pike", and we all joined in. By the time we'd sung through half a dozen songs, everyone had cheered up considerably, but there was still an underlying sadness at the parting that was to come.

Our household would probably be called a strange one by outsiders, but to us it was ordinary. Jimbo and Pablo both came to the ranch with wives, and they each had a little boy. Since Juanita and Rachel both helped Gloria in the house, it was a natural thing for the three families to eat together. Rachel had once called us a crazy quilt family because of our different races, but that was not a drawback in the eyes of any of us, and we sure enough didn't care what other people might think. The household benefited from the different cultural backgrounds, and we all enjoyed a peaceful home life.

## Chapter Four

We left the next morning before daylight, taking a cavvy of horses with us, with Spooner driving the chuck wagon. By full daylight we were past Walnut Springs and well on our way. We figured to cross the Brazos south of Fort Belknap and set up a base camp on a creek Hutch had heard about.

It was at least an eighty-mile trip, but I thought that even with the wagon we could make it in two long days, or three at most. We encountered no problems until we neared the Brazos River, and then we saw a dust cloud in the north headed our way. For some reason that dust bothered me. "Hutch," I called, and he rode up beside me. "Send Bill out of one flank and Pablo on the other, and tell them to stay in the brush with their rifles ready until we see what's under that dust cloud."

"Right, Earl," he replied and road back to position the men.

The two boys had been riding up close to me, and I told them to go back behind the chuckwagon and stay there. I didn't know what was going to happen, but if it turned into gunplay, I didn't want them to get hurt if I could help it.

I could now see that the dust was being kicked up by a group of riders-- looked like ten or twelve. They didn't ride in any kind of order, so I was pretty sure they weren't soldiers from the fort. We kept on going, but the group swung to stand in our way. I threw my right arm up to call a halt, and a rough looking man on a grulla horse rode up to me. "Where you headed?" he asked in an insolent way.

"Goin' to New York City, heard it was just over that rise up there," I replied in a sarcastic way. In Texas, some questions were down right unfriendly, and asking a man where he was from or where he was going could be answered with lead.

"Smart guy, huh?"

"Smart enough to know that where I'm going is none of your business. Now, get out of the way!" With men like the one in front of me, I'd learned long before to never show weakness, and to drive right at them.

One of the men behind the talker reached for a gun, and that was a mistake. I heard the boom of a shot from Spooner's Spencer, and the man toppled off his horse. That opened the ball, and I pulled the Colt out of my waistband and shot the man in front of em just as he was trying to aim. Down he went, and gunfire seemed to roll across the prairie like thunder.

The outlaws' horses were milling around, and the dust boiled up. They were shooting, but most of their shots seemed to go wild, and before long that ones left on their horses turned tail and ran back the way they'd come.

Our two flankers had been in the right position to take several of the outlaws down, and when we counted, we discovered that six of the strangers were on the ground, all dead. Normally I would have had graves dug and buried them, but I had a hunch their friends might be going back for reinforcements, so I called out to the men that we were going on, and that we did.

When we got to the Brazos, it was up, but we tied some logs to the sides of the chuck wagon and floated it across. Spooner had a four-horse team, and three of us stayed on the upriver side with ropes tied to the wagon box, and with a minimum of trouble we had the wagon across and didn't get our beds wet. Having the river between us and that bunch that had attacked us was a good thing, and while we'd keep our eyes open, I didn't intend to let that mix-up keep us from our goal.

The camp we chose was a good one on a clear creek, with a large flat just to the north where we could hold the cattle we caught. The three boys, Davido, Moses and Britt, had done some skylarking on the way, but they turned serious when we got into camp. They had been pushing the horses along, and when we circled them out on the flat, I assigned Britt and Moses to wrangle, and released Davido to pair with Pablo in the brush. All of us older men smiled at the way he strutted in front of the other two boys.

Early the first chilly morning I laid out the plan Hutch and I had decided on. We would make a long ride to the south, and string out from east to west in a line to sweep as much country as possible. "Anything that turns back, don't chase. There'll be some real old brush hunters in there, and I don't want anyone tying onto one of them and getting a horse hurt."

Red spoke up. "What about us riders? Don't you care if we get hurt or not?" Everyone laughed.

"Now, Red, you know that there never was a day when you were worth more than a good cow horse," I replied with a straight face, and Bill nearly strangled with laughter.

When the laughter at Red's expense died down, I finished. "We'll pair this way: Pablo and Davido, Bill and Jimbo, Red and Hutch, and me and Henry. Moses and Brit will wrangle the horses and tend the cattle that we bring in. Of course, they'll also help Henry when he comes in to cook. Any questions?"

There were none, so we all waited while Bill, the best roper on the L Bar, even though he only had one arm, caught horses for us out of the cavvy. Each rider held onto a piece of the long rope that surrounded the herd until the horses were roped out. Once we'd saddled, the boys took charge of the cavvy, and the rest of us headed south in a group.

We hadn't gone far when we began to see cattle. This was a fairly open area with rolling hills and a scattering of mesquites and low brush. In this dry country there wasn't enough moisture for many plants, though the tough gramma and buffalo grass would put beef on a critter as long as it wasn't overgrazed.

I figured that a good hour had passed when I stopped and swung around. The pairs of riders rode away from me and Henry until they made a long line, and then, at my arm-waving signal, passed on by those that could see it, we began to ride north at a walk. Cattle flushed, holding their long-horned heads high and strutting out in front of us. We let them pick their own pace, but kept them headed north. After while the outriders on each side began to pull forward until we formed a rough shallow U, and when we came near the camp, we moved closer and began to push the wild animals, for that's what they really were, to keep them from turning back.

With only eight of us, we couldn't close all the gaps, and some of the old mossy horns slipped away, but what we mainly wanted was young stock anyway. Of course, the cows with little calves we let go as they would only slow the drive down. Also, any bulls that wanted their freedom got it. By the time we got to the bed ground we had formed a circle around the small herd, and when Britt and Moses joined us, we rode around them at a slow pace, crooning and talking to them, hoping they'd settle down. I counted about thirty head of good beef in the bunch.

The plan was to let this group settle before we added to it, and that would take the rest of the day. One man of each pair went to the cavvy and roped out a fresh horse, coming back to relieve the other man to do the same. Henry went to the chuck wagon and stirred up a fire to heat beans and beef for supper.

When all of the riders had fresh mounts under them, we continued the circle. The cattle were beginning to settle down now, and the sight of men on horses didn't seem to bother them much anymore.

By nightfall we were in pretty good shape. Hutch set night guards, assigning Henry and me as last guard. That way Henry could start breakfast if everything was quiet whole I watched the cattle. Once we'd eaten we pulled our bedrolls out of the wagon and it wasn't long before all but the herd guard were asleep.

My father had told me about catching wild cattle in the Big Thicket and other brushy parts of Texas east and south Texas, but I'd never experienced it. There they made exciting moonlight rides, charging through the brush with a small loop held down low, and making quick throws as a ladino crossed a clearing. Catching those critters was only half the battle, for once caught they would fight anything and everything around them. Often, a thirteen hundred pound steer had to be yoked to a tame ox or a burro to bring him in.

In open country, such as we were working, things were done differently. The first bunch of cattle was tamed down some before we added to the herd. By the second day, we felt like we could leave them with the herders and go after more. This time we went west, and the country was rougher with lots of draws and dry creeks crossing it. We couldn't hold a line like we had done before, so we spread out in pairs, and began to scour the brush and low places.

I pointed to a brush choked draw and Henry and I headed for it. We dropped down over the edge and started to work our way south. Suddenly, with a crashing of brush, a cow and a young bull headed for the bank. "I've got the bull!" I shouted to Henry, and he peeled off after the cow.

That young bull was a fine animal, and once we changed him to a steer, he'd sure enough do for the drive. I was riding Sunny, the dun mare that Pablo had trained for me out of a wild herd, and she hunkered down to gain on the fast moving critter. I built a loop in my rope and waited until we were in range, and then swung once for momentum, and threw at the bull's horns. The rope settled, and I tapped Sunny side with a spur. She put on a greater burst of speed and crossed behind the bull, and I flipped the rope down to settle just above his hocks as we swept past, dallying hard on the saddle horn.

Sunny swung to the left, the rope pulled tight and, down went the critter in a cloud of dust. Before the critter knew what was up, I was off the horse and had a short rope on three hooves, tying him so he couldn't get back to his feet. This one was too wild to drive back to the herd, but we'd brought a couple of burros with us, and I brought one of them out and tied the bull to him, after sawing the sharp tips of the bull's horns off. The burro was fed grain at camp, and while he was a nuisance around the cook fire, he'd earn his feed by dragging the young bull in.

By the time I'd gathered my rope, I could hear Henry calling me, so I went back through the brush and found him on the edge of the draw with the cow down. She wasn't old enough to be called a mossy horn, and she didn't appear to be either nursing or carrying a calf, so we figured we could drive her. Henry left his rope around her horns, and we headed back to camp.

For several more days we scoured the area until it became hard to find cattle close in. One evening I talked to Hutch after supper about moving. "Earl, we've got two hundred and twelve head, and we've either got to move to a new catch area, or go back home. What do you think?"

"With no more men and horses than we've got," I replied, "I reckon we might as well head for home. When we get back we've got to work these critters and gather whatever we can on the place. Then I figure to take a page out of Colonel Goodnight's book and buy enough extra cattle from ranchers around us to make up a herd of two thousand."

"We're goin' up the trail with two thousand critters? That'll take a lot of men, eighteen or twenty. Where you goin' to get them?"

I thought about that for a bit. "When we get home, how about you going to Fort Worth and hire about fifteen? I want to take Henry to cook, and Davido, Moses and Britt to wrangle horses. Then I figured on you for trail boss. That leaves Jimbo, Pablo, Red and Bill at home to look after things. How's that suit?"

"I reckon it'll do, but are you sure you want to be saddled with three boys on a trip like that?"

"Well, I've been watching those boys, and they're young and not real cow smart yet, but they all three seem to learn fast, and they don't shirk. Pablo's been bringing the other two along like he's done with Davido, and with you as trail boss, I figure they'll do fine."

By the stars it was just after midnight when Hutch spoke my name. My eyes flew open, and I asked, "What's up, Hutch?"

"Got a Comanche feelin', Earl. Haven't seen anything, but the horses are nervous."

"Which side of the herd?"

"South side."

"Okay, wake all the men, and tell the boys to get under the wagon with their rifles. When we're all saddled, you take two around to the east side, have Pablo and Jimbo go north, and I'll hang on here with Henry. Tell the boys to mount and stay with the cavvy."

"Right, boss." He slipped off and began to wake the crew.

I had kept Crowbait up as my night horse, for he could see well in the dark, and now I saddled him and led him to where Henry was waiting beside his own mount. I whispered, "Let's mount and move slowly around the camp, keeping an eye on the horses."

The hours seemed to drag, but finally there was some color in the east, and dim daylight bean to spread across the land. Henry and I were a little ways north of the wagon, and we could look out across the herd. We saw riders slowly circling the cattle, and when we looked at the cavvy, the horses were all looking off to the south, their ears sharply pointed.

The Comanches were masters at deception, and I had a hunch they might have split up. Since the wind was coming from the south, they might want us to think that's where they all were. "Watch to the north and west, Henry. I've got a hunch those in the south are a diversion."

Hutch rode up to the boys about then and motioned for them to move the horses closer to the camp. Henry and I had our rifles out and we were watching to the northwest, where the morning light was slow in coming, when we heard a whoop and saw Indians rise up out of the grass and head our way. I fired my rifle and a Comanche hit the dust, but there was no way of knowing if I'd really hit him. He may have dropped out of sight to wriggle closer.

Glancing over my shoulder I saw that the Hutch and the others were in a tight circle with the chuck wagon and the horse herd on the inside. The cattle would have to fend for themselves, though I doubted if the Indians would pay much attention to them. It was horses they were after, and if it was a large raiding party, we would need a lot of luck to keep them off.

Now mounted Indians, six in number, came charging from the south, but Henry and I kept our eyes on the northwest. I could hear the guns of the others banging, and as I looked at the spot where the warrior I'd shot at hit the ground, a group of Comanches rose up out of the grass and ran toward us.

Henry had dismounted and was shooting across his saddle. I saw one of his heavy bullets hit an Indian and knock him back. The problem was, Henry's rifle was a muzzleloader, and it took time to reload.

I was firing fast with my Henry rifle, and I knew I hit at least two of the Comanches, though how badly I didn't know. The grass was long where they had hidden, and when one of the Indians dropped, he could not be seen.

Four Comanches kept on coming, and they were close. I dropped the rifle, catching the leather strap on the saddle horn, and drew the Colt from my waistband. Out of the corner of my eye I saw that Henry was also using his revolver. Three of the Indians dropped, and we both fired at the remaining one at the same time.

Together then we turned and looked to the south, and we saw two Indians running their horses away. We rode to the group around the chuck wagon, and Hutch reported that we had no wounded. It was a miracle, and the first time I had ever fought Comanches that they had not inflicted death or injury. "We were lucky, Hutch," I said, and he agreed.

Henry started a fire for breakfast, and the rest of us went out to the herd and began to gather them in. Not many had strayed, and the Indians had paid no attention to the cattle, so we were in good shape. We did not go looking for Comanches in the tall grass. We knew that as soon as we moved off, the Indians would come back and pick up their dead and wounded, and hunting injured Comanches in tall grass and brush was like looking for a grizzly bear armed with a switch. If you were unlucky, you might find him.

As soon as we'd eaten, I sent Hutch and the rest off to begin driving the cattle, and Davido and I stayed to help Henry get ready to roll. "You babysitting me, Mister Lamar?" Henry asked with some sarcasm.

"Could be," I replied. "Cooks are hard to find out here in the mesquites."

He chuckled, and went on loading things up. When he was ready to roll, we moved off at a trot. I figured the Comanches that got away from the aborted raid would be coming back with their friends before long, and I'd just as soon that all they saw of us was our dust.

Hutch had moved the herd slowly, and we came up to them in a short time. I took the point and we headed for home, thankful that we were all in one piece. When we crossed the Brazos we kept an eye out for a possible return visit from some of the scum we'd run off on our way out, but no one appeared.

We got back on a Friday, and the homecoming was real fine for all of us, but particularly for the married men. Glory hugged and kissed me so often while I was putting things away, that I finally sat down on the small couch in our bedroom, and we snuggled up. Ralph had been asleep when I got back, but he was soon awake and up on my lap. Ah, it was good to be home.

The ladies planned a big outdoor meal for Saturday in celebration. Juanita, Rachel and Henry were going to bury a side of beef with hot coals and have a real Mexican barbeque, and the three ladies had been baking pies for several days, so we wouldn't run out of good things to fill our stomachs. I sent Moses into town to invite Elmer and Flora for the meal, and told him to stay over and come back with them.

On Saturday morning Bill and Pablo had the other two boys working on the horse herd. They wanted to make sure that any sore backs or brush scratches were tended to. Hutch would head for Fort Worth on Monday to scare up some more cowboys for the drive, and being the best foreman a man could have, I had no doubt he'd come back with some good hands. In the meantime, he and Jimbo began to go over all the saddles and other horse gear to make sure anything with too much wear would be replaced before we left.

By late morning when Elmer and Flora Wilson arrived in their buggy with Moses riding by it, the tables were groaning with food. I helped Flora down and she went on over to the tables to add to the burden.

"How'd you do on the drive?" Elmer asked. "Moses said you came back with some cattle."

"Pretty good, though there are a lot of slick cattle left out there. When we get back from Kansas I may hire a bigger crew and go back out."

"When will you head north?"

"Probably a week from Monday. Hutch is going to Fort Worth to see if he can rustle up some hands next week, and when he gets back, we should have everything ready to go. We start gathering our own cattle Monday. Sean O'Sullivan and Miss Hattie Groves have already finished their gathers, and they'll help us so it shouldn't take long. Together we'll probably have over a thousand, but I'd like to have at least two thousand to make the trip worthwhile. I figure if I put the word out, I might be able to buy some from the ranchers around here to make up the extra."

Now the triangle began to ring, and men and boys headed for the tables in a rush. When Elmer and I got there, Gloria came up and gave us both a kiss. "Will one of you men ask the blessing?"

I nodded at her dad, and he took off his hat, as did the other men, and we all bowed our heads. "Lord, we sure thank you for being with Earl and the crew that went out to gather wild cattle. Now, they're getting ready to go north with a trail herd, and we ask that you go right along with them. And would you please bless all this fine food that's been prepared for us, and the hands that have prepared it? Amen."

We lined up at the tables, and soon talking quieted as we addressed the good food. As things settled down, Henry began to tell the story of our Comanche raid, and as he told it the facts became distorted to the point that I didn't recognize the telling, and I'd been there! He made it funny rather than dangerous, and we all laughed at his embellishments.

Later, after we helped the ladies and Spooner clean up, Elmer asked to speak to me in private, so we went into my office. "Earl, who are you leaving here on the ranch with the women and kids?"

"Ha! Now, that's a question that I have an answer to, but believe me it hasn't been a popular on in some quarters. They're already howling about it, but this time I'm going to leave Jimbo and Pablo, along with Red and Bill.

The last two don't have any interest in going, and the first two are family men. Why do you want to know?"

"After our interrupted trip to Fort Worth last year, things have been pretty quiet around here, but I've heard the Reconstruction people are kicking up a fuss down in Austin, and the new general in charge is going to send out representatives to every sizeable town to make sure we're all doing what he wants us to.

"Now, a friend down in Waco wrote me that General Griffin's friends are grabbing every piece of land they can get their hands on. Seems like they went to the courthouse and went through the records, and if there was any irregularity in the tax rolls, they immediately started action against the owners to seize their land for non-payment. I know you've already had some trouble along those lines when that crooked banker and his stooge tried to take your place, and it might happen again."

"Well, we'll cross that bridge if and when we come to it, but what does that have to do with who I leave behind?"

"The men you've named are all fine, and they'll keep things going here as well as protect the ladies and kids, but what about a legal representative? Someone who can go to bat for you at the courthouse, if need be?"

I thought about that, and I could see what he meant. I might need someone to stand up for me in court while I was gone, and none of the men I was leaving behind quite fit that bill. "Elmer, have you ever heard of a 'Power of Attorney'?"

"Yes, I have. It gives the person named in it the power to act in legal matters for another person."

"Well, would you serve as my Power of Attorney while I'm gone?"

"Of course I will, but wouldn't you rather have someone that knows more about the law?"

"No, I don't think so. You know me, and you have a vested interest in this ranch, since it supports your daughter and grandson. I think you'd be just the right person for the job. How about it?"

He laughed at the reference to his "vested" interest. "All right, if that's what you want."

"Good. Monday I'll come in and we'll get the papers drawn up. I'm sure Judge Smallview can advise us on the proper procedure."

We left it at that, and later when I told Gloria about our conversation, she agreed that her father was the best person to have the Power of Attorney.

Sunday after church, as we were visiting out in the churchyard, I let it be known that I was buying cattle. "How much you payin', Earl?" Cordell Stewart, a rancher east of town asked.

"Eight dollars for full grown steers delivered at the L Bar. I don't want anything under two years and no heifers, cows or bulls."

"How much you figure to get when you reach Kansas?" he asked.

"As much as I can, and a little bit more if possible," I replied with a grin.

Stewart slapped his leg and laughed at that one. "Well, I'll bring you some cattle and take your eight dollars each. You can have the profit when and if you get them to the railroad, and all the expense and trouble that goes with it."

He had been gathering cattle already, and he promised to have about one hundred head to the L Bar by the following Friday. There were two other ranchers there in the churchyard who said they'd bring small bunches as soon as possible. Money was still scarce in Texas, and I figured I'd make up a trail herd without much problem.

When we got back to Elmer and Flora's for Sunday dinner, Elmer opened his hidden safe so I could get some money out to pay for cattle. "Henry will be in to buy trail supplies this week, Elmer, and I'll settle with you before we leave."

"That's fine son, or you can wait until you get back to settle up. I've been laying in more supplies since the ranchers around have made a little money on cattle, so Flora and I are doing fine."

I grinned at him. "Elmer, you're a good friend, and not a bad father-in-law on your better days. Still, I like to keep things paid up, so I'll come in and settle before I go."

Elmer and Flora only had one child--Gloriaa-and since we married, they'd treated me like the son they'd never had. They would have been good friends without the family connection, but with it, they were even better. Of course, since Ralph was their only grandchild, they'd probably have treated me well even if I'd been a saddle tramp.

The next days went by in a whirl. We gathered our own cattle, cutting out steers for the drive, and at the end, along with those I bought, we had just over two thousand head. Now came the hard work of branding, first the calves born since the fall gather that would stay on the ranch, and then the wild cattle from Throckmorton County and the ones brought in from other ranches.

Finally, on Friday, April 12, 1867, we finished the work and were ready to head north. Friday night Henry and helpers, following a Mexican recipe suggested by Pablo and Juanita, lowered a burlap wrapped half a beef deep in the ground on a bed of green oak posts above red hot coals, covered the meat with head sized stones and old boards and then heaped dirt on it. Twenty-four hours later it would be dug up and eaten, a pleasure to all who partook.

On Thursday I had left the final branding to Hutch and the crew he'd brought back from Fort Worth, and gone into town to invite friends out to the ranch for the Saturday feast. The one the week before had been for the ranch people, but this time we were going to invite anyone who wanted to come.

Saturday morning the women kept the kitchen hot all morning baking bread, pies, and cakes. Out in the yard Henry had a large washtub filled with potatoes, boiling away on an open fire, while he stirred a huge pot of gravy. The good smells alone made a man's stomach growl with anticipation.

Elmer and Flora were the first to arrive, and I helped carry several large bowls of her light bread rolls into the house. When I went back out, more folks were coming from town and the neighboring ranches. By the time Henry and the boys dug the beef up, tables made out of long boards on saw horses were groaning with food, and kids were running around everywhere.

I had made it a point to invite Pastor Carl Wilhelm to the party, and he brought his wife with him. The church in Meridian had grown in the last year to a point that it needed a full time pastor, and Wilhelm had been appointed there. Just recently his wife had come from Jefferson in East Texas to join him.

"Earl, I'd like you to meet my wife, Trudy," he said.

I pulled my hat off and welcomed her to the L Bar. "Y'all make yourselves at home."

Out of the corner of my eye I saw Gloria coming my way, and turned to introduce her to the pastor's wife. "So happy to meet you, Mrs. Wilhelm," she said, and immediately led her off to the kitchen where the other women were gathered.

I took the pastor around and introduced him to the other men, and he and Sean began to talk about people they knew down near Waco.

Before long we all met around the tables. Pastor Wilhelm, at my request, thanked the Lord for the food and good company, and we began to fill our plates.

There had been some Indian trouble out in Tom Green County, and Hank Beard was telling Red about it when I came up to them. Red said, "Earl, it's been quite a while since we've had a raid around here, but I'll see to it that we're ready when you and the rest are gone. I have a hunch that the bunch that jumped us out west were just some young warriors feeling their oats, since they weren't very smart, but if not, they may come calling."

"Thanks, Red. Gloria will help you get the guns in the house ready, and you know the rest of the drill, so no problem. We won't have a lot of horses left here, since we'll need most of them on the drive, so they'll fit in the barn pens where you can keep an eye on them, just in case."

I remembered the last Comanche raid not long after I returned home from the war. It was just after some friends and I had rescued Elmer and Judge Smallville from jail, locked up by a renegade former Yankee captain. Elmer had gone back to the ranch with me where his wife and daughter--my Gloria--were, and the Comanches had attacked one early dawn. We'd beaten them off without any serious injuries on our side, and that had been the last raid.

Of course, Comanches being the kind of fighters they were, there was always an outside chance of an attack, though more and more people were taking up land on the western edge of Texas civilization, and that seemed to keep the Indians pushed back.

As we ate, the sound of voices rose and everyone seemed to be having a good time. The food was disappearing at a fast rate, and the women and Henry looked pleased that their efforts were appreciated.

## Chapter Seven

Sunday was the final day the men going on the drive had at the ranch, since Monday morning early we would start the herd north. All three families wanted to go to church that day, so we set out in two buggies. It was a bright day, not too hot, but with plenty of sunshine. The mesquite trees were just leafing out, and it was real pretty to see the sunshine filtered through them.

In town we split up, Jimbo and his family were headed for their church in the south part of town, where Pablo would drop them off and take Juanita and Ramon to the Catholic Church. I headed our buggy to Wilson's store where we met Flora and Elmer. The team was unhitched and turned into the small pasture back of the house, and we all walked to the Methodist church, with first Grandma and then Grandpa carrying Ralph.

"My, he's getting big," Flora said as she passed their only grandchild to Elmer.

Gloria laughed at them, and replied, "He eats enough for two, so he should be big." Ralph was growing like a weed, and I wondered how different he would look when I got back from the drive.

Leaving my family at home while I pushed two thousand head of cattle up the trail was not to my liking, and I had already decided that after this trip I would send Hutch or someone else to ramrod all any herds we sent north, and stay home. But this one was perhaps the most important for the ranch, as the money received would set us up for several years' worth of expenses, and I felt obligated to go myself the first time on the new trail.

"Leaving in the morning, Earl?" Elmer asked.

Gloria turned her head away, but I knew a tear would be glistening in her eye. "Yep, first thing," I replied in a voice that I hoped would convey to my father-in-law that he better change the subject. He took the hint.

"Gloria, I'm going to make soap next week," Flora said in the silence. "Do you and Rachel and Juanita want to come in and make it a party? I've got all the makings, and with four of us we ought to be able to turn out enough for a year for both households."

"Why, that sounds good, Mom, but can you put all of us up?"

"Of course I can. We'll put pallets down for the little boys, and with the spare cot, the three of you ladies can share your old room."

Elmer chuckled at this comment. "And I reckon I'd better go sleep in the barn."

"Oh, no, Dad," Gloria said quickly. "We'll need you around to baby sit, and lift heavy things." She smiled sweetly at him, and he shook his head. There was suddenly an ache I my heart, and I longed to be in Elmer's shoes.

After church, we stood around outside and talked with the neighbors for a while, and then went on back to the Wilsons' for dinner. I could tell Gloria was having a problem keeping the sadness away, and I wasn't doing much better myself. Finally, I said, "Glory, and folks, I want you all to know that I've made up my mind this will be the last cattle drive I go on. When this one is over, and I'm back home for good, I'm done traveling. I'll hire a trail boss or send one of the men from the ranch, but I'm not making any more trips."

Gloria beamed at me and got up from her chair to come and kiss me, and both Elmer and Flora voice their approval. The rest of the meal was happier, and when the other L Bar families came to meet us, we headed home in a lighter spirit.

The next morning before daylight I hugged Gloria to me and went to give a sleeping baby a goodbye kiss, and then I was gone. Long goodbyes always made things tougher, and I went right out to catch up my horse and head for the herd.

Henry had breakfast going, and I ate with the men, and then switched my saddle from Crowbait to Sunny, my first day horse. There was just a hint of pink in the eastern sky when we began to chouse the cattle, getting them on their feet and moving. The four men who would be staying behind came out to help us start the drive. They would stay most of the day, and then go back home before dark.

I wondered which critter would take the lead, and as I was near the front on the windward side, I could see pretty well. At first the leaders kind of swapped places and bunched a little, and we had to keep them headed, but then I looked back and saw a big red steer--must have been over six years old--with an enormous rack of horns prodding cattle out of the way and moving up toward the lead.

I remembered that steer, for he was one of the wild bunch we'd brought in from Throckmorton County, and he had led all the way to the ranch. Pablo called him Jefe, and it looked like he was going to be "the chief", no matter what the other cattle thought. After a half hour of pushing and hooking his way forward, he took his place proudly in front of the herd, pointing to the north. Now, the cattle seemed to feel easier, and they settled into a sound trail gate, not too fast, but covering ground.

That first day's drive was not long. We headed them northeast toward Fort Worth, intending to hit the Chisholm Trail north of that town around Gainesville. A man in Meridian had told me about the trail Jesse Chisholm had forged through Indian Territory and on to Abilene, Kansas where the railroad had loading pens. The railroad was building on west, but a town had grown up around the pens, and cattle buyers waited there to buy the cattle brought up the trail from Texas. After a confirming letter from Captain Murphy Sorrel, a Yankee soldier, but also a friend in Fort Worth, I decided we'd try that route rather than going to Baxter Springs.

Before sunset we rounded the herd and stopped them in a grassy bowl with a creek running nearby emptying into the Brazos River. A soon as we stopped, I asked Pablo, Jimbo, Red and Bill to go on back to the ranch. With no slow cattle to follow, they could make the trip back in a short time, and I didn't want the women left alone too long after dark.

"Mister Earl," Jimbo said, "Rachel told me that Miss Gloria told her this would be the last drive you would make, is that right?"

"It sure is, Jimbo. I don't like being away from my family, and after this time I don't think I'll have to."

"Well, me and Pablo been talkin' about that, and we think we'd like to make one long drive too, maybe next time."

"Uh-huh, and have you discussed that with Rachel and Juanita?"

"No, sir, we haven't. Being a married man, you know that wives can make things miserable for their husbands if they don't exactly agree with what a man wants to do. We figure it'll be time enough to tell them when the next drive comes up." Pablo came up as we were talking.

I laughed at this bit of married wisdom, and replied, "Okay, you two, I'll tell you what. You can both go on the next drive, but you'll have to make it right with the women. That's not my department."

I was chuckling as they headed back to the ranch with smiles on their faces, but I knew that when the time came for the next drive, they might not be so happy. One thing I had learned in my short time as a married man was that not all of my decisions met with my wife's approval, and she had a way of changing my mind, and I was pretty sure it was the same for Pablo and Jimbo.

The herd was quiet during the night. Hutch had assigned me and Alex Knowland, one of the men he'd hired in Fort Worth, to the last watch from four o'clock to daylight, and we rode around the bedded herd until we could see a little bit of light in the east, and then headed back to camp. Henry banged his triangle just as we came up with the horse herd. Davido was the horse wrangler this morning, though that would change as I had detailed all three boys to change off. The ones not wrangling would be driving the drags.

As Davido brought the horse herd together, two more of the new men-- Lafe Nodding and Angel Arroyo--came out with the big rope to make a temporary corral. Since Pablo and Bill, our two best ropers, were back home, I was the next best, and I stepped off my horse and pulled my rope off the horn string. When the corral was formed, I went in to the horses and roped each cowboy's pick as he called them out.

There is an art to roping horses, and not all ropers have it. To begin with, the roper stays on the ground rather than on a horse. Then there is the loop: to make a rope sail out ahead of a roper on horseback, the rider twirls it around his head until it has gained enough momentum, and then lets it go to drop over the horns or head of a critter, or drop down to the heels for a foot catch. But twirling a rope in a horse pen only excites the horses and makes them try to get away, so the roper trails his loop behind him, and when he's in the position he wants to catch a horse, he quickly lifts the loop and sails it out to drop over the horse's head. If the distance is great enough that the rope needs extra momentum, the roper might give it one quick twirl, but no more.

I happened to have the knack of roping horses, so first thing in the morning it was up to me to catch the mounts for each rider.

Finally, after catching the horses the men pointed out, I caught Sunny for my day horse, and turned the bay I'd been riding, named Salty because he was, back with the herd. Salty was a good quiet night horse, but he had a mind of his own--the reason for his name--and while he was gentle to work around, because Pablo had trained him, he would cold jaw from time to time.

When a horse cold jaws, he hangs onto the bit and won't pay any attention to what the rider wants him to do. That can cause some interesting wrecks, but Salty had a weak spot that Pablo had discovered. He hated to have his ears fanned. Whenever any of us felt him grab the bit, we would take off our hats and slap his ears, and he'd let go.

Sunny, on the other hand, was well named, not only for her light yellow color, but also for her disposition. She was a mare out of the first bunch of wild horses we'd caught, and Pablo had put a finish on her that fit her personality and made her as gentle as a kitten. Normally, mixing mares with geldings wasn't a good idea because when a mare came into heat, the other horses, even though they were geldings, would fight each other for her favors, but Sunny was good about that, too. Her heat cycles were short, and she rarely made a fuss or caused one.

That day we pushed the cattle some to get them well off the home range and wear them out for nighttime. Hutch had us drive until early evening when we came to a slough where the animals all watered. The cattle were tired enough that they ate little before settling down for the night. I had first watch that night, and Hutch was riding around the cattle in the opposite direction. We met on the side away from the camp and paused for a word. "They seem real quiet, Hutch."

"Yeah, but have you noticed the lightning flickering off in the southwest? If that storm heads this way the critters may not be so peaceful."

I looked off to the southwest and saw the flickers he was talking about. We called it heat lightning, but in reality it was just so far away that we only saw a little residue of a storm either building or in full bloom over the horizon. "Well, I reckon we can't do much more than wait and see if it comes our way."

With a nod, Hutch carried on and so did I. The cattle didn't seem very nervous as they would have if a storm was coming close, but that didn't mean much. In Texas and other planes states, a storm can pop up at any time without warning. Those storms are ones drovers dread. At ten o'clock by the stars, Alex and Angel came out to relieve us. By that time, thankfully, the lightning in the southwest had died down.

I rode ahead on the third day out, and found the sleepy village of Gainesville right where folks said it would be. Off to the west there was a large flat with good grass, and I decided we'd bed our cattle there. A creek flowed north along the western edge toward the Red River.

As I guided the herd onto the bedding ground, a storm cloud that had been steady in the northwest all day began to move in our direction. It was swollen with rain, and when it came closer, we could see lightning flashing. Hutch came up and said, "I'm putting six men on each guard shift tonight. If that storm hits, we may have trouble holding the cattle."

"Good idea. I assume you'll be checking from time to time, so I'll do the same."

Henry served up a good hot meal with plenty of biscuits. "Take some of those sinkers with you tonight, boys," he said. "If that storm breaks you may not get another hot meal for a while." He was right, and we all knew it. Henry drove the chuck wagon, and he had a young helper--Eduardo--who drove the bed wagon. Eduardo Nunez was a young man--seventeen years old--that Hutch had hired in Fort Worth. Captain Murphy Sorrel, a Yankee soldier, but a man that had become a friend to all on the L Bar, had recommended him since he knew the boy's father, and Eduardo had turned out to be a very good hand.

The two wagons were usually set in such a way that they helped to shelter the fire and those who gathered around it, but for tonight, they were side by side, their tongues pointing north, and the teams that pulled them were staked out nearby. Henry knew that he and Eduardo might have to leave in a hurry.

I had my night horse staked close, and it was reassuring to hear him munching the good strong grass. I'd unsaddled him, but left my rig right close by. Darkness came, rent from time to time by lightning flares, and I pulled the top flap of my bed up over my head and went to sleep in the handsome bedroll two of the ladies of the L Bar had made me.

Just before I left on a cattle drive to the Pecos River, Juanita and Rachel had surprised me with the finest bedroll a man could ever use. I was the envy of every cowboy on that drive and everybody else who saw it from then on. The bed was canvas covered with buttons along one side like a shelter half. The inside was covered with wool blankets sewn right onto the canvas so they couldn't slip, and there was a canvas flap to pull up over my head in case of rain. It was a wonderful bed.

I came awake thinking it must be after midnight, though there were no stars to tell time by. The storm was closer, thunder rumbling and lightning flashing in a steady rhythm. I had only removed my boots and hat when I lay down, so it was no trouble to dress and throw my saddle on Crowbait, my steadiest night horse. As we trotted out toward the herd, a great crash of thunder filled the night with sound, and as the lightning came down, I saw it strike the ground not far away. Suddenly the cattle were on their feet and running.

I had been in a small stampede once when we had a gather that ran in a thunderstorm at the ranch, but never anything like this. I was near the front on the river side of the herd, and I tried to push them right, but they were wild-eyed and fast. Lightning hit the ground again on my left, and the smell of sulfur was strong. Suddenly, I saw balls of blue light dancing from horn to horn on the cattle as St. Elmo's fire set up a ghostly trail, and they tried to run faster.

Again I was thankful to be mounted on Crowbait, for he was as sure footed as a mountain goat. My mind flashed back to the Louisiana lady who'd given him to me after I had rid her house of an unwanted guest. That was not long after the war ended, and a lot of things had happened since, but

Crowbait was still a good horse. Of course, he was nothing to look at, and I often thought there might be some camel in his background, or maybe a moose, but tonight I was glad I was up on him.

The herd hit a deep gully, and it slowed them some. I jumped Crowbait over a couple of struggling steers and climbed the bank ahead of them, staying on the edge and pushing the cattle that came over off to the right. If I could get some of them to turn back they might mill and come to a stop.

Suddenly, out of the gloom of rain I saw a rider, and then another. They came up out of the gully and began helping me push the cattle around. Some steers pushed by us and kept on at a trot, but we let them go, concentrating on the large group, and it began to work. The rain was heavy now, but the lightning and thunder had moved off. As the three of us pushed the cattle back to the east, more riders came up and soon we had them in a mill. "Back off!" I called to the men with me. "Let 'em settle."

When the cold, wet dawn came, we saw that while we had a sizeable bunch in our circle, there were a lot more unaccounted for. Henry came up with the wagons and started a fire under a flysheet, using dry wood and cow chips from the cooney under the cook wagon. Hutch left four men with the herd, and came to the fire to eat. "There's two dead ones down in that gully, and two more with broken legs," he said. "Looks like we've got about half the herd in the gather, so I reckon we'll have to comb the country to come up with the rest."

"Why don't we leave the boys to ride herd on what we've got, and the rest of us spread out and gather what we can? We're not far from the Red River, and I have a hunch it's on the rise this morning, so we'll gather cattle until it goes down enough to cross."

"Sounds right." He finished his meal and quickly began to give orders. After we roped out fresh mounts, the three teenage boys, Britt, Moses and Davido threw the remuda in with the cattle and began to ride slowly around the herd. Some of the steers were lying down, but most of them were on their feet, browsing at the grass. I didn't think they'd run again for a while, though I had heard the horror stories about herds that were infected by the urge to run, and they'd stampede every night at the same time if not watched closely.

I rode off straight to the Red River to see what it looked like, and sat my horse on the south bank watching the water boil and tumble down the channel. The river was still rising, with uprooted trees and clumps of brush sailing by. I saw some dead cattle go by too, but I didn't think they were ours. Turning back I began to collect cattle, but they were hard to drive for one man, so I waited for help with a herd of about thirty. I sang to them and slowly rode around them, and they settled. In a couple hours Hutch came up and together we pushed the steers back to the growing herd a few miles south of the river.

Salt Creek was flowing strong though bitter, and we'd found a good holding ground west of it. Luckily, the grass was high there, and the cattle showed no signs of wanting to wander. For three more days we gathered cattle. At one point I rode east for a couple of miles and came upon some strange cowboys scouring the brush. "Lose many?" I asked as I came up.

The man that seemed to be in charge answered, "Had three thousand until the storm came and they broke. Looks like we're still missin' four of five hundred. How about you?"

"We had two thousand, give or take, and we've found most of them." I reached out and shook hands with him. "Earl Lamar, L Bar on the Bosque."

"Logan Miles," he replied, taking my hand. "Rafter Eight, Trinity River."

We talked a bit more, and then went our separate ways. When I got back to the herd I called Hutch over and said, "Let's go look at the river, Hutch. The Rafter Eight is about four miles east of us, and I'd like to get across before them if possible."

We'd been keeping an eye on the river, and it had been going down, and today, the sand banks on both sides were now visible. "What do you think?" Hutch asked.

"I think we ought to try it. I've got a hunch there'll be quicksand on both sides, but if we keep them moving, we should be alright." The spot where we were was known as Red River Crossing. It was the best place to cross for miles due to the low banks on each side, and other herds had used it before us. "You wait here in case I get bogged down, and I'll see what it's like."

I stripped down to my long underwear and sat Sunny to the water. I'd ridden her through creeks and small rivers several times, and she was unafraid, but when we got past the sand bank and into the deep channel, she'd have to swim, and I didn't know how she'd handle that. I needn't have worried though. She stepped right in and swam about twenty yards until the riverbed sloped up and we rode through the sand banks on the north side.

Once we'd turned and gone back, I stepped down and dried off as much as possible with my shirt, and then dressed. "What time do you want to start?" Hutch asked.

"Let's head them up at daylight and come right on up. I think with two men on each side, and one of us at the point they should do okay. The rest can push the cattle on in, keeping them moving."

"How about the wagons?"

"We'll take them over first so Henry can have a hot meal ready when we're all across."

We were all up early the next morning, and just at daylight we pushed the steers off the bed ground and pointed them north. When we reached the river I asked for four swimmers to guide the cattle, and quickly rejected Moses, Britt and Davido. "I want you three on the drags to keep them moving." Alex, Angel, John Smith and Ad Newell volunteered, and I took the point.

We held the cattle back when we reached the river while we hitched four horses to the chuck wagon and took Henry across. He'd piled all the supplies up on boards that he'd brought along for the purpose. These boards were set above the bed about a foot, so any water that came in shouldn't get them wet.

We all stripped down to long underwear, wearing our hats, of course, and I led the wagon out with the four outriders keeping ropes taught on both sides. The crossing was made without incident, and we quickly went back to bring the bed wagon across in the same manner. Henry moved both wagons up stream away from where we'd bed the cattle, and promised to have a hot meal ready as soon as possible.

Back on the south side, I swung my hat in a circle and Hutch, who was with the herd, answered the same way. As Jefe came to the river bank, I led out and he followed like a pet dog. We'd all been giving the lead steer pieces of bread and other goodies from time to time, and he was almost tame, if that word ever applied to a longhorn.

The cattle took the water with no trouble, and the four outriders kept them moving in the right direction, while the rest of the hands pushed them in. The trick was to keep them all moving together. Cattle like to be with their fellows, and they are easiest to handle when close bunched. I changed from Sunny to Crowbait just before noon, and as Hutch took over from me when I reached the north bank, I went over to Henry's wagon to dress and have a good steak with boiled potatoes, and about a gallon of hot, hot coffee.

"Comin' to the end, boss?" Henry asked.

"Getting close, Henry. We should have them all over by mid-afternoon."

"Good. Eduardo and I will have a good feed ready."

Chapter Nine

After talking to Henry, I rode over to check on the men that were loose herding the cattle that had already crossed. Richard Howard and George Nightham, two of the new men Hutch had hired in Fort Worth were slowly riding around the herd. Since they had everything under control, I decided to go back to the river crossing and see if I could lend a hand there, but I stopped when I looked at the hills off to the north I saw a group of riders headed our way.

Of course, we were now in Indian Territory, but the riders didn't look like Indians, and as they came closer I could see that they weren't. George came around the end of the herd and asked, "How do you want to handle it, boss?"

I thought for a minute. "Have Richard ride back and get some more men, and then you ride off about a hundred feet and lay your rifle across your pommel. If shooting starts, you'll know what to do." He nodded and went to talk to Richard.

As the group came close to the herd, I held my right hand up and called out, "Who are you and what do you want?"

They came to stop about twenty feet from me, ten rough looking men. The leader was in front, and he spoke through a bushy black beard, "Now, that's not a really friendly greeting. You own these cattle?"

"I do."

"Well, you're goin' to need help crossing the Territory, and we're offerin' it to you."

"I see, and why would I need help to cross Indian Territory?"

The man grinned and I could see his yellow teeth through the whiskers. "Why, there are all kinds of bad men over here, and most of them don't like Texans, so for a hundred dollars and a hundred head of beef, we'll help you get through."

I laughed at him. "Have you tried to pull this stunt before, or is it the first time?"

"Makes no difference. You pay or we'll just go ahead and take your herd anyway."

"With only ten men? I don't think so."

"Oh, we've got more than ten." He took off his disreputable hat and waved it above his head. Behind him more men appeared on the low ridge, ten or twelve more of them.

"How good do you think they'll be without you to lead them?"

"What do you mean?" he asked. I could see I wasn't dealing with a fast thinker.

I pulled the Colt out of my waistband and centered it on his stomach. "Because, as soon as somebody starts the ball I'm going to let all the air of you, bushy beard."

"I've got the two on his right, boss," George called out. The herd cutters looked to the right and saw him standing behind his horse with a rifle laid across the seat of his saddle.

The men on the ridge were drawing closer, and I could see that if George and I were going to come out of this with whole skins, we'd have to take charge before they arrived. As I looked at the leader, he whipped out a revolver, so I tilted the Colt and fired, hitting him in the right arm. He howled, and the others began to fire at me and George as their horses milled around.

I shot at the man behind the leader, and then swung to touch one off at the man on the other side. Over the sound of revolver shots I could hear the deep boom of George's rifle, a Spencer .56 caliber, and saddles were emptying. A shot took my hat off, and another one nicked my left shoulder, and fire behind me began to rise in volume. I glanced back and saw Hutch leading the way with our cowboys spread out behind him.

The second group of outlaws had just arrived when the L Bar came running, and the herd cutters quickly, and wisely, turned tail and ran, trailed by the others who could still ride. I stopped our crew, and checked for wounds. George had not been hurt, and my nick was just that, hardly more than a scratch. None of the others had been touched. We'd been very lucky.

We looked over the downed outlaws, and found that four were dead, and two wounded, including the leader that I'd shot first. We tied the wounded to their horses and sent them back to where they'd come from, and got shovels to bury the dead. They didn't really deserve it, but I took out my Bible and read a psalm over them, and then we went back to the cattle.

While we were fighting off the herd cutters, the boys had continued to push the last of the cattle over, so we rounded the herd and placed four guards around them, and then went to the chuck wagon.

The next morning we lined them out just at daylight, headed north toward trail's end at Abilene, Kansas. Now came the endless days and nights on the trail. The drive I'd made to New Mexico on the Goodnight-Loving trail had taught me what to expect, but except for Hutch, none of the others had ever driven cattle any distance. It was nine-tenths a boring, tiring job, and one-tenth a harrowing, dangerous, heart quickening time if the cattle ran or Indians or herd cutters tried to take the cattle.

Three weeks on from the Red River crossing, we came to a small village on the Canadian River, although village might be too fancy a name for the half-dozen brush shacks. I had Hutch throw the herd off to the east as I scouted along the river for a good crossing. I found a low bank with some deep wagon ruts and assumed that's where other herds had crossed, but to make sure I rode down into the water and splashed my way across. From the look of the marks on the banks the river was way down, and it looked like the crossing spot would work well, the cattle not even having to swim.

Back on the south bank I swung my hat in a circle, and Hutch pointed the herd my way. Henry was on the windward side and he came up with Eduardo following in the bed wagon. "I think you can go right across, Henry. There's a channel in the middle about two feet deep, but no quicksand. Do you want to wait for some outriders?"

"If you'll lead, we'll try it right now," he replied.

I was riding Jake, a dark bay that Pablo had trained, and he was a real water horse, so I turned him and headed back down the river bank. Henry came right after me, and Eduardo followed. We crossed the wagons with no trouble, and I went back to lead Jefe and the herd into the water. It was the easiest crossing we'd made so far, and when all the cattle and horses were across, I looked over the river at the shacks and saw a familiar face...the bushy-bearded leader of the group that tried to cut our herd on the Red River. Now what was that no-good doing up here?

Sometimes I get hunches or maybe glimmerings of future problems, and I had one now. The man I was looking at was trouble, and since I'd seen him twice now, I also knew I'd see him again somewhere along the trail.

During the war my hunches or strange ideas had saved my bacon and other's too more than once. One moonless night I woke up with a feeling of impending trouble, and I spoke to the captain. I don't know if he had a feeling too, or he decided to trust mine, but he got the troop up and we quietly moved several miles to the north of our overnight camp leaving one scout behind to see what happened. When daylight came, the scout appeared riding hard to report that a Yankee company had surrounded our camp and rushed in to attack just at daylight. So, we set an ambush for *them*, which worked out well for our side, and from then on the captain always paid attention to my hunches.

Another thing I'd learned in the war was that there was no sense worrying about what might happen in the future. Once you've made all the preparations possible, you have to let events take their course. If that man in the bushy beard decided to make trouble, we'd just have to handle it.

When Hutch came up I told him about seeing the bearded outlaw, and he said he'd pass the word. "You think we should have extra guards tonight?" he asked.

"Yes, but let's do it bit differently. Leave the four close in on the cattle, and have two or three more ride a circle a quarter mile out from the herd. They can give us an early warning if the herd cutters try anything."

Hutch agreed and gave the men their night orders. I ask him to put me on the two to four o'clock stint, and I rolled into my bed to get what sleep I could. One thing about cattle drives...no one ever got enough sleep.

When Hutch woke me up, it was as dark as the inside of a cave. The moon was new, but that didn't matter anyway, since the sky was overcast. I saddled Crowbait and rode out to the herd by sound. The men had been told not to smoke or make any light, so I had ridden part way around the herd before I came up to one of them, and then I'd have missed him if I hadn't heard the slight jingle of his bridle chain.

"Who's that?" Lafe asked.

"Earl," I replied. "Seen any sign of trouble?"

"Ha! Haven't seen anything at all for an hour. You come to relieve me?"

"Yep. Go on back to the wagon."

"Well, that's fine, but where *is* the wagon?"

I chuckled at this comment. It was so dark nothing could be seen from horseback. "Climb down, and come up to me."

We stood shoulder to shoulder and looked off the way I'd come from. A half dead tree could just be seen pushing high branches into the sky, a darker mass than the darkness around it. "Head for that tree. When you get there, look off to your right, and you'll see the coals of Henry's fire."

He moved off and I began to circle the herd slowly, going more by the sound of the cattle than by sight. Crowbait had good night vision, but I wondered if even he could see anything in this darkness. Before long I came to Angel Arroyo riding toward me. We identified ourselves and both reported no trouble of any kind. "But, Senor Earl, I feel a storm coming on. How about you?"

"It does seem awful humid," I said. "Right now I wouldn't mind a little lightning to give us a look at the herd, but only a little." He chuckled, knowing full well that nature never let us decide how much we received of anything.

We parted, both riding on at a slow walk. In a few minutes I came to Hutch riding toward me. We stopped and talked for a few minutes, and then rode on. Crowbait had only taken a couple of steps when we heard the roar of thunder close overhead, and I got my wish for lightning, only not a little bit. Most times lightning would come in forks or streaks, but this came as a huge fireball in the sky, right over the herd, and the crashing thunder never stopped.

In an instant the cattle were on their feet and running, and I rode as quickly as possible to the near edge, trying to keep up and stay in the saddle at the same time. The ground was fairly smooth where we'd bedded them, but off to the north it was broken up by shallow ravines, and north was the way they were running.

Chapter Ten

The darkness was gone now, replaced by the weird flashing light all around. At least the cattle were not running headlong, but they were steadily plunging along as if they had a goal in mind. I held Crowbait to a long lope, reached the point of the herd, and tried to push some of the leaders off to the west to get them slowed down. Luckily, there was very little rain with the thunder and lightning, and I could see the herd clearly.

We came to a shallow gully with sloping sides, and it slowed the stampede considerably. I spurred Crowbait up the far side and was able to get ahead of most of the front rank, pushing the leaders off to the west. Up ahead I could see some riders off to my right, and looking back I saw more behind me on the east side of the herd. The cattle were slowing now, many trotting, with some dropping to a walk. Finally we got them turned westward enough that they all walked and after a bit more travel the whole herd stopped together. The stampede was over, and it hadn't been as bad as the one on the other side of the Red River.

I guessed that all my crew had jumped to help in the stampede, for there was a large group of riders slowly moving around the herd. Some of the cattle began to graze a bit, and a few were lying down in the thin drizzle that had begun to fall. The lightning and thunder had moved off, but a gray dawn had come, so I could see for quite a ways.

Hutch came up to me and said, "Earl, I've been all the way around, and I don't think we lost many. Do we drive or hold for today?"

"Let's hold today, get a count and let them settle, and we'll point them up first thing in the morning. Have you seen any strange riders around at all?"

"Nope. Are you thinking about the low-life you shot?"

"I am. I don't care much to kill anyone, but I think I should have overcome my objections where that one's concerned. I thought I heard a shot about that time the first clap of thunder dropped down on us. Tell the men to keep an eye out for strangers today, and to let you or me know immediately if they see anyone hanging around."

"Will do." He swung his horse and rode back down the line. Henry had set up his cook wagon not far off, and I headed that way. As I neared the fire, I saw the boys bring up the horse herd. By this time on the trail the horses were broken in to the routine, and while they had mixed some with the cattle in the run, Moses, Britt and Davido were smart boys, and they had immediately begun cutting the horses away from the cattle as soon as daylight came.

I changed saddles to Sunny, letting Crowbait have a rest after the hard night, and then went to the cook fire. "Henry, keep your eyes open for strangers. If anybody shows up and neither Hutch or I am at the fire, send Eduardo to find one of us."

"Okay, Earl, and I'll keep old Betsy handy, too," he replied, patting the double-barreled shotgun leaning against a wagon wheel.

"What do you have the cannon loaded with?"

"Well, let's just say if it goes off, make sure you're behind it." Eduardo laughed at this comment, and I grinned. Henry was known to put some peculiar things down the barrel of the gun, like horseshoe nails, salt, and bacon rind.

"How about you, Eduardo?" I asked. "Do you have a gun?"

"Si, Senor Lamar." He dug into his bedroll and pulled out an ancient cap and ball Walker Colt. It was big and heavy enough to wear wheels.

"Where in the world did you get that cannon, Eduardo?"

"My uncle picked it up on the battlefield in the war with Mexico," he replied, and I didn't doubt him. "He said he was right behind a Texan, a ranger, who was shot dead, so he exchanged his smooth bore musket for this Colt and fought on."

"Well, be sure and hold it with two hands if you have to shoot," I said.

The Walker Colt was named for the man who first commissioned it-- Samuel Walker, a Texas Ranger and captain of cavalry in the Mexican War. He wanted a long-barreled six-shot repeating revolver of .44 caliber that could be carried in a holster on a saddle, so that his men could pull it out in a hurry, and one powerful enough to take down a horse, if need be. Walker helped design the gun. Unfortunately, Captain Walker was killed in the war a few days after receiving a presentation pair of the weapons from Samuel Colt himself. Walker never really got to test the gun named for him, but other men used it to their satisfaction. Not many were made, and even fewer were still around, but occasionally one surfaced as this one had.

By afternoon the cattle were grazing and the men that had spread and searched had brought in all the strays they could find. There were only about thirty head in the last bunch, and doing a rough count, Hutch and I figured we had about all of the cattle that had run. "We were lucky to have so many men out with the herd," he said. "The outriders heard the noise and came in to help the night men, and as soon as the sound reached those of us in our beds, we were in the saddle, so the stampede was about over before it began."

We were discussing the cattle when I looked off to the southeast and saw a group of men approaching the fire. "Hutch, looks like we've got company again. I'll go to the fire, and you alert the boys around the herd, but keep at least four of them out. The rest you can bring in slowly."

"You figure it's our old no-friend with the beard?"

"I do, and if he starts something this time, I think I'll shoot a bit straighter."

Hutch went off on his errand, and I rode slowly to the fire, arriving just about the same time as the group of riders. The bearded one was about to dismount, when Henry whipped up the shotgun and said, "Don't get down! State your business, and then get out!"

"Now, that's not real friendly cook. We just dropped by for a cup of coffee."

"It's not hot," Henry said, motioning to the large pot sitting next to the fire and, steam gently lifting out of the spout.

I had ridden up behind and a bit on the right of the group, and I spoke up, "All of you can leave except the man with the black beard. I want him to stay."

They were startled at my voice, and some of them started to turn their horses. "If you turn your horses, have your hands filled, because I'm going to start shooting as soon as I see a horse's eyes," I said in a soft voice.

Now all movement stopped. Henry and I had them boxed, and they didn't like it. Still, some might have taken a chance, but Eduardo came around the corner of the wagon at that moment holding the Walker Colt in both hands, with the hammer eared back. His hands were shaking just slightly, and he said, "Senor Earl, I am not very steady. What happens if this gun goes off?"

"Why, Eduardo, the size that bullet is, it'd probably kill two men." The men around bushy beard were frozen. "All of you except bushy beard, slowly, and I mean very slowly, drop your weapons on the ground. Start with your belt guns, and then your rifles. Do it now!"

I watched as revolvers hit the ground, followed by a collection of rifles. When the last weapon dropped, I said, "Now, all of you except bushy beard, turn your horses and ride away at a trot."

They complied just as Hutch arrived with all the men except for the four he'd left with the herd. "Eduardo, Henry will keep bushy beard covered. You gently ease the hammer down on that cannon." Now his hands weren't shaking, and I wondered if he'd made them shake on purpose to worry the herd cutters. He was one smart boy.

"What are we going to do with bushy beard, boss?" Hutch asked.

"Why, we could just shoot him, I suppose, though that seems kind of low. I know, let's get him down off his horse and see what he's made of." I put my gun up and dismounted, watching as the outlaw stepped down off his horse.

Bushy beard was keeping his hand well clear of the gun holstered at his side. "Now what, mister?"

"Well, you've been followin' this herd ever since the Red River, and I'm pretty tired of it. I figure you and that trash we sent away had a hand in scatterin' our cattle back yonder, and then you had an idea that you could follow along and one day ride in here and maybe take over the whole herd. Well, that didn't work out.

"Now, you don't deserve it, but I'm going to give you a choice. You're wearing a gun, and so am I. You can go for it and take your chances, or you can drop it in the dust and start walking south. It's early in the day, and I figure if I send a couple of men along to keep you headed in the right direction, you could be several miles from here by sunup tomorrow. What'll it be?"

"Huh. If I shoot you, these others will just cut me down, so what real choice do I have?"

"That's the way you'd do it, bushy, but we're cut from different cloth. Hutch, if he downs me, you let him go. Take his gun and his horse, but let him walk off by himself."

"Okay, Earl. I'll see to it."

"Now, how about it?"

He waved his right hand around in front of him as if he was going to say something, and then it swept down and grabbed the grips of his Colt. It was an old dodge, and not real well done, so I wasn't fooled, but I waited until his gun was clear and he fired, his bullet going into the dirt at my feet, then I palmed my own gun and shot him. This time I made sure of my shot, and it took him in the heart. He was dead before he hit the ground.

Hutch looked at me, and said, "Well, I guess he won't bother us again, will he?"

I turned away, climbed into the saddle and rode back to the herd. I didn't like killing, not even killing a snake like bushy beard, and it always affected me afterward. In a running fight with guns going off all over, it was different, but killing a man standing in front of you felt all wrong somehow.

When I got to the herd, I rode away from the men there, and I saw that Hutch had followed me and was speaking to them. None came near me, and for an hour I rode by myself. Finally, my mind calm, I headed back to Henry's fire, and stepped down off my horse. "Fresh coffee, boss," Henry said, handing me a cup. I took it gratefully and watched as Davido unsaddled my horse and turned him into the cavvy.

The next few days were uneventful. I wondered if we'd see any more of the herd cutters, but evidently with their leader gone, they weren't interested in trying again. We were between the North Canadian River and Cimarron River when the old trapper joined us. I was riding point, and I saw him come out of a copse of trees about a mile away. He sat his horse and waited, and I rode along the edge of the herd to talk, motioning for Lafe Nodding to take the point.

"Howdy," I said as I pulled Sunny up.

He nodded, spat tobacco juice off to the left, and replied, "You the herd boss?"

"I reckon, at least I'm the owner."

"Had any Injun trouble?"

"No, just some no-account white men trying to cut the herd."

"Heard about it," he chuckled. "Buried old George Miller back a ways, didn't you?"

I looked at him and noted the smile in his eyes. "Well, we didn't know his name, but if he was a bushy headed low life, black hair all over his face and head, I reckon he's safe now."

The old man cackled at that. "Not if he went where I figure he did. He's probably pretty well singed by now. Anyhow, you did the Territory a favor when you planted him. But now you got trouble comin' that won't be so easy. Ever hear of Black Band?" I shook my head. "He's a Kiowa, and a real bad one. He made war talk a few moons ago on all white men and their cattle. I just crossed his trail on the North Canadian day before yesterday, and he's comin' this way with a heap of braves."

While he was talking I looked the man over carefully. There was no doubt that he was a trapper. He wore shrunken buckskins and moccasins, and there was what looked like a wolverine cap on his head. His beard was full and grizzled, but it looked like he'd chopped it off with a knife, and the same knife had hacked off some hair. His horse was a sorrel with poor looking lines, but then as the owner of Crowbait, I couldn't talk down any other man's mount. The packhorse behind him was a docile bay, not wearing a halter or lead rope, but sticking close to the sorrel.

I stuck out my hand to him and said, "My name's Earl Lamar of the L Bar down on the Bosque River in Texas."

He took my hand and replied, "Cage, Jim Cage, out of the Shining Mountains."

"Well, Mister Cage, thanks for the warning about the Kiowas. I reckon we'll have to keep our eyes peeled. Would you like to trail along and camp with us tonight?"

"Don't mind if I do."

We went back to the herd, and fell in along the west side. The cattle were so well trail broken by now that they moved along at a good walking gait following Jefe as he headed north. We went on until we came to a creek that seemed to empty into the Cimarron, and there Hutch had the men round the herd and let them settle for the night. I rode to the cook wagon with Jim Cage beside me. When we got to the fire, we dismounted, stripped the gear from our horses, and turned them over to the boys.

Moses and Britt stared at the old mountain man until he whirled around and said, "You boys think you'll know me next time?"

Both of them hung their heads and said they were sorry for staring. I laughed, and so did Cage, and the boys moved off with the horses. We watched as they spoke to Davido, evidently telling him about the mountain man.

That night Jim kept us entertained as we ate and then lounged around the fire. He could spin yarns from cobwebs, and while most of them sounded too wild to be true, at least some of them might have been. I'd heard that these old trappers lived pretty wild.

The next morning when I rolled out of my soogans, I noticed that the old man was gone. It was just before daylight, so I hadn't slept late, but evidently Cage had the urge to move even earlier, and he had quietly saddled his horse, loaded the pack animal, and took off.

The day started as so many had, and by ten o'clock the herd was strung out and moving nicely. I'd sent Lafe out to the left side as a scout for Indians or renegades, and Alvin to the right on the same mission. We had just passed a thick bunch of trees when Lafe came charging toward me, only slowing as he neared the herd. "Boss!" shouted when he got close enough, "There's a whole batch of Injuns coming at a high lope!"

I pulled up, and he stopped his horse. "Now, Lafe, take a deep breath and tell me how many you saw."

As he was calming down I saw Jim Cage come out of the trees and head toward us at a dead run, his pack horse following close to the side of the sorrel he rode. He slowed as he came up, and finally stopped. "Black Band is just on the other side of that walnut grove, Lamar, and he's got about twenty braves with him."

"Painted?" I asked.

"Yep, every one of them."

"Lafe, Hutch is on the other side of the herd. Go on over there and let him know, and warn every hand you come to. Tell Hutch to keep the cattle moving as long as he can, but if shooting starts, to circle them and leave two men with them."

I noticed Henry was out in front with the wagons, and I rode over and told him what was coming. He and Davido pulled their wagons up side by side with a gap of twenty feet left between them. As I turned back I saw them unhitching the teams and tying them to the wheels inside the shelter.

Cage had stayed with me as I rode from place to place, and now he said, "Here they come," in a casual voice. He dropped off his horse, and gave a sharp command. Both animals dropped down to lie on their chests. The trapper laid his rifle across his saddle, and I saw that he was forted up. He fired, and an Indian dropped from his horse.

I preferred to have some maneuverability, and I was riding Sunny, the little mare with the fast feet, so I stayed in the saddle. As the Indians came out of the trees, they spread out into a more or less straight line. It was over two hundred yards from the trees to the herd, but Jim began to fire almost immediately, and every time he pulled the trigger, an Indian went down. He could reload that muzzle-loader almost as fast as I could jack a cartridge into the Henry.

I pulled my rifle out of my saddle scabbard, and when I thought the Kiowas were close enough, I started shooting. Now they split on some prearranged signal, half going south toward the back of the herd, and half heading north toward us.

At the sound of Cage's first shot, Hutch had rounded the cattle into a compact bunch. He and the cowboys he hadn't left with the herd split like the Indians, some around the north end, and some around the south. Cage was till picking off individual warriors, but the lead Kiowas were bearing down on us.

I dropped the Henry back in its boot and pulled the Colt .41 out of my waistband, but I only fired once when an Indian painted with black streaks all over his naked body threw a lance at me. I nudged Sunny with a knee, and she sidestepped neatly avoiding the lance.

The warrior followed up his attack with a knife in his right hand. As soon as he was close enough he launched himself at me, hitting me hard and knocking me out of the saddle, and knocking the gun out of my hand. I landed on my back, looking up at the Kiowa as he dropped down on me, knife arm raised.

There was no way I could get at my other gun, so I grabbed the knife arm in both hands and twisted the Indian off me. Still holding the arm I tried to stand but only made it to my knees. The Indian matched me, also kneeling.

My nose was filled with the wild smell of the Indian, and his black eyes glittered above his snarling mouth. He tried to release the fingers of my hands from his wrist, and when that didn't work, he transferred the knife to his left hand and immediately plunged the blade down toward my chest. Just in time I dropped back and the sharp blade only grazed my arm, though I felt the sting of the point.

Once again I grabbed the knife arm, and this time I twisted to my right, throwing the Kiowa off balance and rolling him under me. The jar of hitting the ground loosened the knife, and I was able to bat it away. Quick as thought he jumped away from me, rolling over and reaching the knife just as I managed to palm the .36 Colt from its holster and pull the trigger. His chest was almost touching the end of the barrel when it went off and he was flung back. The man was dying, but there was no give up to him, and as the light went out of his eyes, he was still trying to swing his arm to throw the knife in my direction.

I rose to my feet and shakily looked around me. Off to the v
retreating Indians, and my men were rounding the end of the he
my way. Cage was sitting cross-legged on the ground not far
coming from a wound in his right arm, but I noticed his rifle w
capped and he was ready. As I looked at him, he spoke and his
back to their feet.

"Looks like we beat 'em off," I said, still trying to recover fr
"You beat 'em off, hoss! That Kiowa you killed was Bla
they'll go mourn for a while, and then pick another leader. P
bother you again figurin' you're bad medicine. They'll wait until
comes along."

The men were coming in now, and I leaned on Sunny w
returned to its normal beat. "Looks like your arm's bleedin',
said.

I looked down and found my shirtsleeve torn, but when I
cut it was pretty shallow. Cookie came over, rolled up my sle
bandage on it, and then bound one around Cage's cut, and I s
else hurt?"

Lafe had a scratch and Angel's horse had a burn along his
than that, we'd come off without a casualty. "We were lucky," I
Cage cackled at that. "That you were, hoss, but your boys
shots, and you're not too bad in a hand to hand fight your own
course, I thinned 'em out some with old Brown here," and he p

Hutch sent one of the men to count the dead Indians, an
get the herd moving, Hutch. If the Kiowas are like the Com
want to come back for their dead, and I'd just as soon not be h
come." Victor came back from counting Indians, and reported
boss--eight along with this one."

"Enough," Cage said. "They'll sure figure you're bad med
clear of you from now on. Not a bad thing."

As the cattle lined out still headed north, I took a positic
and Jim Cage rode along with me. "Want a job, Jim? I can use

He laughed, and replied, "Sorry, Lamar. I like you, and yo
a panther, but I'm too long in the tooth to take another man'
string along with you for awhile though, if you don't mind."

"I understand, and you're welcome to 'string along' with us
want."

## Chapter Twelve

We crossed the Cimarron River two days after the Indian fight, still headed north. Jim Cage said it ought to be about four day's travel to the Kansas line, though we wouldn't really be able to tell. Still, I looking forward to leaving Indian Territory, for I'd had about all the ement I wanted there. According to the word I'd had from drovers at Worth, it was about 140 miles from the Kansas border to Abilene, and country was mostly flat or rolling hills, with only the Arkansas River to . Ten days more or less from the border to the stockyards.

As we neared the mythical border, really only a line drawn on a map where in Washington D.C., the days grew really hot. We'd been on the for fifty-eight days, and it was now June, a hot month in most of the try we were traveling through, though not as hot in Kansas as it was in s. It was also a time for thunderstorms...and they could pop up at any

We saw one more group of Indians before we left their territory. I was g point when I saw a scraggly bunch of horses and people on foot come

up out of a fold in the land. Cage rode up beside me and said, "No Kiowas in that bunch, Lamar. Those are Kaws, and they're sure not lookin' for a fight."

I signaled Hutch to come take over the point, and trotted over with Cage to the Indians, who stopped when they saw us coming. He raised his right hand, palm toward the group, and an old man on a thin spotted horse raised his hand in the same way, and uttered something in a guttural voice. Cage answered in the same language, and the two of them talked with words and hand motions.

Finally, the trapper turned to me and said, "The chief is Man's Horses, and he and his people are headed for the Canadian to try and find buffalo. His people are sick and hungry, and he wonders if you would give him a steer out of your wealth."

I looked at the group, men women and children were all thin and dressed in tattered skins and cloth. This bunch of Indians looked like if they didn't have some help soon, they'd all be dead. The hungry looking little children pulled at my heart, and I thought about the L Bar family back in Texas. We were very lucky to be well fed and clothed.

"No problem, Jim."

I looked at the herd and saw that the drags were going by, so trotted off toward the cattle, and with help from Moses and Davido, I cut out two steers and headed them back to the Indians.

As soon as the cattle got close the Indians saw my intentions, two of their warriors kicked their horses' sides, and ran right at the steers, yelling and waving lances. As the cattle broke into a trot and then a lope, the Indians ran their horses along side and quickly killed them both with lances.

When the steers were down, the women took over, and with flashing knives began to skin the animals out and cut choices cuts to drop in ready pots, while the older children built fires to cook the meat.

I sent the boys back to the drags, and rode over to Jim Cage. He looked at me and nodded in approval. "Good man," he said. "Lamar, I think I'll just trail along with old Man's Horses for awhile. Never lost anything in Abilene anyway." He reached out and took my hand, giving it one hard shake.

"Thanks for your help with the Kiowas, Jim."

The old trapper nodded, and turned his horse away, and as I rode back to the herd, I thought to myself that in a lot of ways he fit the Indians better than he did white men.

The next morning Lafe awakened me for my watch--the two to four a.m.--and I shook out my boots in case of nighttime visitors, and pulled them on. It was the full darkness of an overcast night, with a half-shell moon peeking through from time to time. Once I had my horse saddled, I went to the coffee pot that Henry always had sitting next to the coals, and poured a cup of hot, strong brew. It was an eye opener, and when I finished the coffee, I was ready for my watch.

Skirting the edge of the herd of cattle--most of them were lying down--I came to Alvin York riding toward me. We stopped for a minute and talked, and then moved on, both of us singing softly to let the critters know where we were.

Light was just coming in the east when I heard a rumble of thunder. It seemed to be coming from right overhead, but I couldn't be sure. As I reached for my slicker tied behind the cantle, a shaft of lightning split the overcast and illuminated the cattle. I tensed, knowing that no matter how well trail broken they were, the herd could easily jump to their feet and stampede. But to my amazement, they didn't do that.

Some of the cattle stood and stretched, and a few began to walk around a bit, sniffing at the grass, but as the lightning continued to flash intermittently, I could see that none of them appeared very worried about it. I pulled my slicker on just as the first drops of rain began to fall, and I thought it might be a soaker, but we must have been in the edge of the storm, for the rain only came down for a short time, and then began to slack off. By the time full daylight crept over the land, the rain had stopped and the cattle were mostly on their feet, grazing and looking peaceful.

We lined them out, thankful that they hadn't run, and headed on into Kansas. The next days were uneventful, and we didn't push the herd, letting them graze along and put on weight eating the good Kansas bluestem. Finally, ninety-six days after we left the Bosque, we settled the herd on a good bunch of grass south of Abilene, Kansas, and I road into town to see if I could find a buyer.

The town was new, and that was not hard to tell for all of the buildings were still wearing traces of green lumber--not a speck of paint on any of them. Of course, not all the dwellings and business establishments were made of wood, there were soddies and tents, as well as crude shelters made of flint buffalo hides.

North of the railroad tracks I could see several frame houses that looked more substantial, one or two of them two-storied. I wondered how much that lumber had cost to bring out here to the almost treeless plains.

The smell of the place was not new either. It was to be expected that there was the smell of cattle from the holding and loading opens east of town, but there was also a hard smell of drying flint buffalo hides. The demand for these hides back east had just begun, and there were men out on the plains following the vast herds of Indian cattle, shooting them down and taking the hides, leaving the meat to rot. No wonder the Indians were mad at the whites. In their place, I'd have felt the same way.

I rode up to a building that boasted of being a hotel, though it sure wasn't anything like the hotels I'd seen in Fort Worth. I tied Sunny to the rail in front, and went on into what passed for a lobby. "Any cattle buyers staying here?" I asked the clerk behind a high counter?

"Some," came the short reply.

"Can you name some, and tell where I might find them?"

"How much you willing to pay for that information?"

The man had a Yankee twang to his voice, and an eastern accent, and his look was one of contempt. Admittedly, I didn't look like a prosperous man, still wearing trail clothes that were stained and torn in places, but that didn't give the clerk any right to turn up his nose. "Well, mister, I reckon I'm not going to pay anything in money, but I might pay in knuckles if you don't answer my questions." I said this in a calm, matter-of-fact way, smiling at the time.

The clerk opened his mouth to reply, but a man sitting in a chair off to one side spoke first. "Elmer, you better mind your manners. That man looks like he might just break your New York nose, and then how would you turn it up again?"

I watched as he got to his feet. He was dressed in a town suit, but he wore riding boots, and he didn't have an eastern accent. "Name's Harley Owens, mister," he said, advancing with his right hand outstretched, "and I'm a cattle buyer."

"Pleased to meet you, Mr. Owens. I'm Earl Lamar owner of the L Bar down on the Bosque River in Texas," I said as I took his hand.

"What kind of a herd to do you have to sell?"

"All steers, two to five years old, all beef."

"How many and where are they?"

"About two thousand, give or take, and we're holding them south of town about two miles."

He wanted to go see them right then, and as we headed for the door, I said to the clerk, "The next time I come in here, mister, you better have polished your manners. I'm a real friendly man, but that's because most of my enemies are dead." The clerk's mouth dropped open, but if he had a reply I didn't wait to hear it.

I followed Owens to the livery stable, where he saddled his horse and we headed south. "Now, you might think that old Elmer is a representative of the town attitude toward Texas men, and you'd mostly be right. This town was put together by the railroad, and they imported the shopkeepers and others from eastern states, mostly northeastern. They like the money you Texans spend in their town, but that's all."

"And how about you, Mr. Owens? How do you feel about Texans?"

He laughed easily, and I warmed to the man. "I'm from Missouri, Mr. Lamar, and as you know during the late difficulty, my state was claimed by both sides. I reckon I'm just glad the war's over so I can go on with my business. I will say this, however, I was in the 6th Missouri Union Infantry Regiment, and I had enough fighting against you Southern men to last me a lifetime. And, I've found that the loudest Yankee voices now that the shooting has stopped are those that never picked up a rifle during the war, like your new non-friend Elmer Ustus at the Grand Hotel."

"Well, I reckon we'll get along, Mr. Owens. I was in the 1st Texas Cavalry, and I'm not too happy about how the whole thing turned out, but I'm sure enough happy to back on the ranch in Texas with my whole hide."

We came up to the herd and sat looking them over. "Looks like you took the last week or so to put some flesh on them. That's good, for I can offer you a little bit more." He started his horse and I followed as he rode through the herd, weaving his way around and looking them over good. Finally, he rode to the edge closest to the cook wagon, and stopped. "I reckon you'd like to talk price before we get to the wagon."

"Uh-huh, I would. How much do you have in mind?"

"Well now, you know you're not the first drover to hit Abilene this year, so I can't pay top dollar, but I'll offer eighteen dollars a head."

I chuckled at this figure as if I traded cattle every day of the year, and I remembered how Charles Goodnight had talked to the Indian agent at Fort Sumner in New Mexico. They had haggled all around the figure they finally settled on, and I'd learned something: the first price offered was not necessarily the final price given. "Well, now, if you could get them for eighteen dollars, Mr. Owens, you'd be doing real well, but since you're the first cattle buyer I've talked to, maybe I need to check with some others and see if I can't get a better price," and I turned my horse and headed away at a walk.

"Now, wait a minute, Lamar," Owens said to my back. I turned the horse back to look at him, and he was grinning. "What price did you have in mind?"

"Twenty-two dollars a head."

"Oh, yes, I'm sure you'd like that, but then I'd probably take a loss. I can go nineteen, but that's it."

"Sorry, Mr. Owens, but that's not enough, not after what it took to get them here. Been nice talkin' to you, but I believe I'll check with some other buyers."

He grinned at me, and I waited. Finally he said, "Alright, Lamar, I'll go twenty dollars a head, and that's the best I can do."

I rode over to him and stuck out my right hand. "It's a deal."

He chuckled, knowing that was the figure I had in mind right from the start. "Now, do you want to sell your extra horses, too?"

"No, we'll take those back to Texas with us."

"Okay, when can we get a count?"

"Anytime you want."

"Now's as good a time as any. How about moving the cattle up to the pens? I'll ride ahead and point the way. There's a counting chute there."

I swung my arm at Hutch, who had been watching from a distance. When he rode up, I said, "Hutch, this is Mr. Harley Owens, who's just bought the herd." I turned to the cattle buyer and completed the introduction, "Mr. Owens, this is my foreman and trail boss, Hutch Rawlins." The two shook hands.

"Hutch, let's head them to the pens by the railroad. There's a counting chute there, and we'll run 'em through and get an accurate count. Tell Henry to follow along and we'll camp closer to town."

He turned his horse and went off, and Owens moved out toward the pens. By late afternoon the cattle were counted--two thousand twelve of them--and Owens and I went to the bank. Twenty dollars a head times two-thousand twelve came to $40,240. "How do you want it, Mr. Lamar?" Owens asked.

I'd already thought about that. "Four thousand in cash, and the rest in a draft to the City National Bank, Fort Worth, Texas."  The last time I was in Fort Worth I'd gone by the bank and learned that they had an association with banks in several northern cities, including Abilene, Kansas, and a bank draft would be honored.

I took the four thousand in Federal greenbacks, enough to pay the hands and have some left over for the trip home. The draft I tucked into a zippered pouch in my belt, but not until I was out of sight of everybody.

Owens and I shook hands on the steps of the bank, and he said, "If you bring another herd up, keep me in mind, Mr. Lamar."

"I'll do that, Mr. Owens, but the next herd will be ramroded by my foreman or someone else. I've got a young family at home, and I don't figure to make this trip again."

When he was gone, I mounted and rode to the camp Henry had set up south of the cattle pens on a small creek. The men were all sitting around, and I knew what they were waiting for.

"Well, men, here's the payoff," I said, as they gathered around, "When I call your name, come up to Henry's table and I'll pay you out."

Each man came to the table, and I paid down three months wages, plus a bonus. I encouraged the three younger boys to only take a bit of their money, and let me keep the rest to give them when we got back to Texas. They reluctantly agreed, and I gave each of them twenty dollars. Never having had so much money in their pockets, they felt like the richest men in the world, but I knew that by morning they probably wouldn't have a dime left. Still, even if they wanted to try drinking whiskey, I knew the bartenders in Abilene wouldn't serve them, so I wasn't very worried about that.

Hutch and Henry stayed back when the others were paid, knowing I would take care of them later. When the job was done, I said to the whole crew, "Along with your pay, I want to thank you for your hard work in bringing the herd up here. Now, today is Thursday, and those of you who want to go back with the wagons, we'll head out Saturday morning. In the meantime, I'm told they've got a city marshal named Thomas Smith here in Abilene, and he's kind of sudden on the shoot, so I'd suggest you have a good time, but leave your guns in your bedrolls and take it easy. You older men, I'd appreciated it if you'd kind of keep an eye on the younger ones."

Everybody except Hutch and Henry saddled horses and headed off to the dubious pleasures of the trail town. When they were gone, I paid Hutch, plus a generous bonus, and the same for Henry. Henry went back to the fire and began to put together supper for the three of us, and Hutch wondered, "How many of those boys do you think will be sober by Saturday?"

I chuckled at that. "Probably not over half, and that half will be broke. I remember once in the war when my troop was camped outside of New Orleans, and we were actually paid. Wasn't much, ten dollars as I recall, and that was Confederate. The captain gave several of us a pass to go into town since we were within walking distance, and it took me exactly ten minutes to get rid of my pay."

"Did you get anything for it?"

"Not much. I went to a store to see about buying some new boots or shoes, since mine were in pretty sorry shape, but the storekeeper wouldn't take Confed money, so I left. Then I thought I might as well see if I could find a place to eat that would take my pay. Well, I went to a pushcart on the sidewalk along Canal Street, and the man had something called 'muskrat stew'. I got a bowl for two dollars, but it was pretty bad. I figured that muskrat had been dead a long time before he made it to the stew pot, or maybe the man had just boiled up the hide.

"I asked the proprietor if there was a boot or shoe store that he knew of that would take my money, and he pointed me down an alley. I wasn't far down the alley when somebody hit me on the head and knocked me out. When I woke up the rest of my ten dollars was gone, along with *my* boots!"

Hutch and Henry laughed at the story, and it was funny in retrospect, but at the time I was sure sore-footed and mad as a wet hen by the time I hobbled back to camp. Before I left town I'd staggered back out onto Canal Street to try and find the pushcart owner, but he was long gone, probably off trying to sell my boots, or making another 'muskrat' stew out of them.

Luckily, the next day we raided a Yankee supply depot, and I 'captured' a new pair of boots to wear.

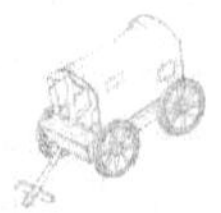

The three of us ate, and rolled in our beds. By the stars it was two a.m. when I was awakened by the noise of someone stumbling around near the fire. Henry shouted, "Hush that noise up and go to bed!" and whoever was making the noise mumbled and moved off. It was not until daylight that we saw three bodies, looking more dead than alive, lying on the ground near the fire.

When we checked them, the bodies appeared to be what was left of Alex Knowland, Lape Nodding, and Alvin York. Henry got their bedrolls down and threw blankets over them. All three looked like they were going to have king-sized headaches when they came to.

Scattered around on the ground was what looked like the rest of the crew. I noted that of the four boys--Eduardo Nunez, Britt Shelley, and Davido were tucked into their bedrolls, so I figured their night hadn't been too wild, but where was Moses?

I shook Britt and asked him. "Boss, he stayed in town. Said he was goin' to get a new hat, and we saw him head for a store. I thought he'd be back by now."

I didn't like the sound of that. Moses was the youngest of the boys, and the most adventuresome, and the fact that he hadn't come back to sleep in the camp was worrying. "What time did you see him last?"

"Must have been about midnight," Britt replied. "We were tired--Ed and I--and said we were coming back to camp to sleep, and Moses said for us to go ahead. He wanted to buy a hat, so we left him there. We met Dave on the way back, and he came with us."

Hutch was listening to our conversation, and he said, "How to want to handle it, Earl?"

I thought for a minute, and replied, "Well, we don't want all hands to hit the town at a high lope, so I think I've got a better idea. You boys get dressed and have a bite to eat, and Hutch, you and Alvin ride in ahead of us and look in the likely places. I'll take the boys with me, and follow you in about fifteen minutes. The first place we'll go is to the marshal's office, then we'll look in back alleys and out of the way places. If it looks like we need more men, we can send back for them."

"Okay, we'll get saddled up and go on in."

Once they were gone, I held the boys back, making sure they were not armed. I was carrying both the Colt .41 and my .36 in the holster, and I hoped I wouldn't have to use either of them, but if anybody had hurt Moses, the town of Abilene, Kansas was going to find out that it was bad business to mess with Texans.

When the time was right, we mounted and trotted our horses into town, going directly to the marshal's office.

Marshal Tom Smith listened to the boys' talk about Moses staying behind to buy a hat, and the store they saw him go into. When they finished, he only asked one question, "He was a black boy?"

I nodded, and replied to his question with one of my own, "Does that make a difference?"

"From your accent, Mr. Lamar, I'd say you ought to know that Negroes aren't real popular anywhere outside Washington D.C. right now. This town is made up of more stiff-necked Yankees than any place you've ever seen, and they sure don't like people of any other color than white, and then only whites born north of the Mason-Dixon line.

"Now, I don't know what happened to your boy, but I'll nose around, and I'd appreciate it if you let me handle this thing. The last thing I need is my jail full of Texans."

He did not smile as he made the speech, and he had a hard glint in his eye. "Tell me, Marshal Smith, how do *you* feel about people of a different color?"

"Got no opinion. I try to treat everybody the same."

"Uh-huh. And how do you feel about Texans?"

Still no smile. "The money you men from Texas spend in this town helps pay my salary, Mr. Lamar, so as long as you and your men behave yourselves, I don't have an opinion about Texans, either."

"Well, I reckon you ought to know that if anything bad has happened to Moses, your town is going to pay, and I don't mean in dollars. I don't believe in threatening anyone, let alone the head lawman in Abilene, but I would suggest you do your best to find that boy and get him back to us unharmed."

He got real quiet; his face took on a stony look, and his right hand moved out from his side. "Or what, Mister Lamar?"

"Or I'll send word back down the trail to the other herds that your town doesn't like Texans. Shouldn't take long before another war between the states starts up, and, Mister Smith, we'll win this one, and we'll bury a lot of Yankees."

He didn't reply, just stood there, so I left it at that and walked out on the porch with the boys. "What now, Mr. Lamar?" Britt asked.

"You boys stick together and ease around to the places you went last night. Don't get into trouble, and leave your horses at the livery stable, tied to the outside fence so you can get to them in a hurry."

They agreed and headed off down the street. I mounted Crowbait and rode up the main street toward the hotel. I had gone only a little way when two men stepped away from the hitch rail in front of a saloon and stood in my path. They looked like some of the down-at-heel trash I'd seen around Abilene, the kind that would be for hire if a man wanted something dirty done but didn't want to soil his own hands. "Would you look at that goat he's riding, Jake," one of them said, a man with dirty yellow hair pushing out from under a ragged brimmed black hat.

The other man, a buck-toothed fellow with smallpox scars on his cheeks, replied, "Couldn't be a goat, Sid. Must be from Texas, and like the rider, maybe just a no account plug."

I pulled Crowbait up when I got within twenty feet of the pair, and I grinned at them. "I call him Crowbait, and he sure isn't much to look at, but he's a mighty fine horse for all of that. Now, here's an interesting thing," I said, raising my voice to be heard by all the bystander, "two of what most folks would call very ugly men, and dirty, too, making nasty comments about a horse that looks better than either one of them. I think you owe Crowbait an apology, boys."

A crowd had begun to gather, and as they heard my words laughter started to ripple around. I didn't take my eye off the two dirty shirts facing me, but I did notice out of the corner of my eye that a lot of the onlookers wore big hats like mine. Several herds had come up the trail behind ours, and their men were in town.

The blond man shouted out an oath and grabbed for his gun. I simply pulled the .41 out of my waistband and shot him. Down he went with a great howl, and his partner took one look at my gun, and turned to run.

The man on the ground was rolling around and cursing, so I knew I hadn't killed him. The crowd murmured, and when I dismounted and went over to the man on the ground, one of them said, "You need some help, friend?"

I looked at him and grinned. He was dressed in clean new range clothes, and he'd been freshly shaved. The dark tan on his face showed some white where his hair had been trimmed, and I knew he was a drover. "Well, yes and no," I replied. "One of my hands, a black boy about sixteen years old, didn't return from this eyesore last night, and I'm looking for him. His name is Moses Alstrom, and I'd sure like to know what happened to him."

"Well, friend, we'll help you look." He turned to several other men around him and said, "Won't we, boys?" There were nods and murmurs from several men on the boardwalk. He turned back to me and asked, "Where do you want us to look?"

"Well, he won't be in the saloons, but you might ask around in them. Then, look in the alleyways and behind buildings. I'm going across the line to look in the areas in the north part of town. I've talked to the marshal, but I don't look for much help from him. A cattle buyer told me that there are a lot of Yankees in this burg that don't like anybody from Texas, and particularly if they're a different color than white."

"Okay...what's your name?"

"Earl Lamar, owner of the L Bar in Bosque County. How about you?"

"Jake Westring, foreman of the M R Connected, Erath County. We'll spread out and see what we can find out, Mr. Lamar."

As they turned away, Marshal Smith came up and looked down at the wounded man still on the ground, moaning now and clutching his chest. "You shoot him?" he asked me.

"Sure did. He had a partner, but he ran off."

"I heard what you said about crossing the line, Lamar...are you looking for trouble with me?"

"Nope, not looking for trouble with anybody, but you know what--that is, who--I'm looking for, and I intend to find him."

Smith looked down for a minute, and then back up at me. "You meant what you said about making war on Abilene, didn't you, Lamar? Well, I guess I better go along with you to see if I can keep the shootings down. I doubt if we'll find your boy around the homes, but you seem bound to try, so let's go." He went into a store and asked someone to go find the doctor for the man in the street, and then he came back out and started up Texas Street along the railroad tracks.

I led Crowbait and walked beside the marshal. This was the first Yankee town I'd been in since the war, and I was certainly not impressed by this spot on the prairie. The most imposing business building was near the stockyards on the east side of town--the Drover's Cottage--built by J.G. McCoy as a welcome to drovers who came up the trail. I wondered if McCoy was a Yankee.

As we neared a sorry looking shack just north of the railroad, I saw a man dart inside that looked familiar. "Marshal Smith, I believe the man who was with the one I shot just entered that shack," I said, and he stopped and looked long at the building.

"Okay, Lamar, you go around back and I'll go right up to the front and call the man out."

I headed off at an angle, and the marshal walked right up to the shack, calling out, "Whoever is in there, come on out without a gun, or I'm coming in!"

I reached a point where I could see both the front and the back of the building, and I stopped there. Slowly, the door opened, and the dirty man I'd seen run from the fight in town came out. "I don't got no gun, Marshal!" he cried out in a scared voice.

Smith had not pulled his weapon, but he walked up to the man and motioned for him to turn around. When he did, the marshal produced a pair of handcuffs and placed them on the man's wrists. "Now, Harvey," he said. "Tell me why you and Walters tried to shoot Mr. Lamar."

I came on up and listened. "'Cause Mr. Hawkins in the Alamo Saloon paid us to."

"Did he say why he wanted you to shoot me?" I asked.

"N-n-no. He just gave us each ten dollars and said when we were done, to get out of town." Ten dollars...not much money for a murder, but then this man didn't look much brighter than a prairie dog, so maybe it was a lot of money to him.

"Looks like we need to talk to this man named Hawkins, Marshal," I said.

"Yes, it does. Let's put this fellow in jail, and go see the man."

I saw the foreman of the M R Connected when we got back to Main Street, and I told him what we'd found so far, and where we were going. "Fine, Lamar, I'll go with you." He signaled to some of his men, and called out, "Curly, take the rest of the men and surround the Alhambra. Don't let anybody in or out."

"Right, boss."

Marshal Smith didn't look too happy about the impromptu posse, but there wasn't much he could do about it. With my men and those from the M R, not to mention other Texas hands from the trail herds coming up that we could round up, we could tree Abilene in a heart beat, and Smith knew it.

When the three of us walked into the Alhambra Saloon, we saw a man in a black gambler's suit slip through a door in the back of the large room. "That's Charlie Hawkins," the marshal said, and he strode right across the room looking neither right or left, and hammered on the door. "Hawkins! Come out here! We want to talk to you!"

A muffled voice replied, "I've got nothing to say to you, Smith, except, you better remember where your paycheck comes from."

"Is he payin' you, Marshal?"

"He and all the business people contribute to my pay, but no one is above the law. I'll just go on in and bring him out." And he opened the door and walked on in. The man's bravery was amazing, for anything could have happened, but before long he came out holding Hawkins by the arm.

With us trailing him to the door, Smith walked through the room, out the batwings, and off to the jail. I looked at the M R foreman and said, "Lets' give this place a shakedown and see if my hand is here." He nodded, and we split up, Westring going to the porch in front of the saloon and calling some of his men to come in and help.

The patrons in the saloon watched us, but no one made a move to stop us. I went back to Hawkins' office and looked around. There was another door in the back of the office, and I opened it and looked inside. This was evidently Hawkins' living quarters, for it contained a bed and table, with a chair shoved under one edge. There was a large closet standing on one side, and I opened the doors, but found only clothes hanging there.

Back out in the main room, I looked up the stairs to the room above, but Westring and one of his men were searching there, and it didn't look like they'd found anything.

I walked over and looked at the bartender standing behind the bar polishing a glass. "You see everything that happens around here," I said in a conversational tone, "So, did Hawkins or someone else bring a young black man in and hide him somewhere?"

The bartended gave me a surly look, and didn't answer. My patience had run out long before, so I lunged over the bar and grabbed him by the shirtfront, pulling him back over with me and holding him there while I shucked my gun, cocked the hammer, and ground the end of the barrel into his ear. His eyes rolled in fear, and I said, "I asked you a question, mister, and I expect an answer!"

"I-I," he stammered.

"Try again."

"L-look in the room behind t-the bar," he got out.

I released him and shoved him into the shelf that ran along the wall. "Show me," I said with my teeth clenched.

He turned and pushed a lever, and a door opened in the wall. I was around the end of the bar in a hurry, and pushed the bartender through the door ahead of me. There was Moses, tied hand and foot and lying on the floor. He had a gag in his mouth, which I quickly removed. "Thanks, boss," he said. "I reckon I was never so glad to see anyone in my whole life!"

I handed the bartender my knife and watched as he cut the ropes that held Moses. He was some shaky when he tried to stand up, but once he'd stamped some feeling back in his legs, we left the room, taking the frightened bartender with us.

Jake Westring was coming down the stairs as I pushed the bartender out into the room. "Found him huh?" Jake said.

"Yep. They had him in a secret room behind the bar. I had to wring it out of this low-life, so I'm going to take him over and give him to Marshal Smith. Thanks, Jake, for helping out."

"Anytime, Earl. You'd do the same for me."

"That I would, my friend."

Moses and I marched the bartender over to Smith's office and delivered him. "This man knew where Moses was," I said, "and I had to shake the information out of him. I reckon you can charge him with kidnapping just like Hawkins."

Smith kind of bristled at that. "I'll be the one who decides about charges," he replied.

"Fine, but the next time the L Bar comes up this trail, I better not see these two out free on the streets, or I'll come right to you, Marshal Smith, for an accounting."

That didn't sit well with Smith and anything might of happened, but then Hawkins yelled from his cell, "You better let me out of here right now, Smith! This is false arrest, and I'm going to get you fired!"

The marshal's face changed, and he gave me a look that said, "See what I have to put up with?" as clearly as if he'd spoken.

I grinned at him, and nodded as Moses and I left the office. The other cowboys were waiting outside, and we mounted and rode back to the rest of the crew.

Chapter Fifteen

Friday morning we rolled out early and over breakfast I asked Henry if he needed any supplies for the trip south. "A few, boss, but I can take care of that today."

"Good. Tomorrow morning we're going to head south and get away from this smell on the prairie. Now, anyone--except you three boys--that wants a last day in town, have at it. I'd avoid Marshal Smith if I were you, but I doubt if anyone will give you trouble. Take it easy, though, and don't start anything."

Alex, Lape and Alvin had all decided to stay in Kansas for a while, so they cut out their horses that morning, shook hands all around, and headed for town. They'd heard that a bunch of men were going out to hunt buffalo for the railroad, and thought that might be an interesting adventure.

Some of the others went into town, but by suppertime, all were back. We ate some more of Henry's good cooking, and soon all were asleep.

Saturday morning we had a late breakfast, and then rounded up the horses we were taking back home, and headed out, with Henry and Eduardo in the two wagons, and the other three boys herding the horses and Jefe along behind. I had learned that many drovers sold their wagons at the railhead, along with their extra horses, but horses and wagons were in short supply in our part of Texas, so we decided to take them back home with us.

I liked the idea of heading back to Texas, for I was missing Gloria and little Ralph a lot. Plus, by now I would have another child to hold, for Gloria was due to have a baby in early June, according to her figuring. I found myself urging Sunny to trot and then lope, and Hutch had to call out, "If you wear your horses to a nubbin, you won't got home any faster, Earl."

I pulled back to a walk, and grinned at him. "You're right, you old bachelor, but if you had a wife and little boy and a new baby waiting for you, I'll bet you'd be pushing hard, too."

Henry laughed at that, saying, "Who could Hutch ever find to marry *him*, boss. Why, she'd have to be blind in one eye and not able to see out of the other one."

"Look who's talkin'," Hutch replied. "I don't see you havin' any luck finding a girl."

"I could if I wanted to," Henry replied in an offended voice. "I'm still young, and there are several young ladies I've got my eye on. Now you, on the other hand, are so old and set in your ways, even if you could find a woman your age that wasn't married with ten or twelve kids, she'd never be able to house train you."

They went on in this vein for some time, but I dropped back and asked the boys how they were doing. Moses flashed a wide grin and replied, "Just fine, boss. Since you got me out of that room, I've felt like I could reach up and touch the sky."

Around the campfire the night before, Moses told us how he came to be kidnapped. He'd bought his new hat and left the store, planning to head right back, but then he thought he might as well buy some candy for the trail home, so he walked up the boardwalk toward the candy store, just on the other side of the Alhambra saloon.

As Moses was passing the saloon, two drunk men--town men from the look of them--stopped him and shoved him off the walk and down into the street. Now, Moses was a smart boy, and as far as he knew he didn't have a friend in town. He'd already heard some comments about his color, but then he'd heard those all his life, and he wasn't about to show the anger he felt. So, when the men pushed him off the walk, he tried to go on past them in the street, but that wasn't enough.

While the men were abusing him, Moses noticed a well-dressed man come out of the saloon and stand on the porch. "Buffalo him, boys!" the man cried out, and one of the drunks pulled a gun out of his pocket and hit Moses on the head, crushing his new hat down over his ears. Down he went, not quite knocked out, but dazed enough to not be able to resist. Someone, he thought it was the man on the porch, tied his hands, and the three of them picked him up and hauled him around behind the building. There he was left in a woodshed, bound hand and foot, and with a gag over his mouth.

Later that night, after he had more or less recovered from the blow on his head, the bartender and Hawkins hauled him out of the shed, untied his feet, marched him into the now closed saloon and locked him into the room behind the bar, after retying his legs. And that's where he stayed until I rescued him.

"What were they planning to do with you, Moses?" Hutch had asked.

"Well, that saloon owner really hated colored folks, and he said as soon as y'all left town, he was goin' to take me out in the country and hang me."

"Just because you're black?" Britt asked.

"Yep. Said all blacks were no good, and he was goin' to hang as many as he could as long as he lived."

We had all pondered on this, and then Henry spoke up. "Moses, it doesn't matter to us what color your skin is, you're an L Bar hand, and one of us. Anybody ever tries to hang you, he's going to have to walk through the whole crew." The rest of the hands all agreed with Henry's words.

Moses had ducked his head, and the talk moved to other things to give him time to recover. I figured there were tears in his eyes at Henry's comment about family, but I hadn't looked real close.

"I see Jefe is leading the horse herd just like he did the cows," I commented, watching the spotted steer stepping right out with the horses pointed up behind him.

Britt laughed, and replied, "He sure is, Mr. Lamar. Even Crowbait stays out of his way. He tried to nip old Jefe in the rear, and that steer whirled like a cutting horse and frapped Crowbait in the ribs with one of his horns. There was a squeal from the horse, but he dropped back and didn't try anything on Jefe again."

We all laughed, and Jefe just marched on, head held high. Lead steers like Jefe were always in demand by drovers, and a well-seasoned one would often go for a higher price than a well-trained cow horse. There was no way we would have let him go to the slaughter house.

We camped that night on a creek not far from a bedded down Texas herd. Hutch and I rode on over after supper to be neighborly, and we discovered that the drovers were out of Somerville County, not all that far from the Bosque. The owner of the HLM Connected was not with them, but the trail boss, Elvin Bennett, was also the ranch foreman, and he asked about prices in Abilene. "We got twenty dollars a head for ours, but the price may be down some now, for we were among the first, and quite a few herds came in while we were there."

"Well," Bennett said, "I'm sure enough ready to get rid of this herd at any price. They took to running south of the Red River, and they liked it so much they've pretty well ran all the way across Indian Territory."

I could see that the cattle were thin and not in good shape. Bennett figured to let them graze on into Abilene and try to put some weight on them, but if they ran as often as he said, they might be just as thin when they reached the railhead.

We visited for a while longer, and then went back to our camp and rolled into our soogans. Evidently the HLM cows decided not to run that night, for when we were eating a late breakfast, the herd was stretched out and headed north.

For three more days we had a peaceful trip, covering twice as many miles or more than we'd done coming north with the cattle. The Arkansas River was down and no real trouble to cross, but when we got to the Cimarron, it was a different story. We hadn't had more than a shower of rain in the days we had traveled, but evidently there had been a heavy one somewhere in the northwest, for the Cimarron was running bank full. I was impatient to get home, but not so impatient that I wanted to try and swim that rushing river, so we camped on the north bank and settled down to wait until the river went down.

We had a quiet night, and the next morning we were all surprised when Jim Cage rode up, slouched in his saddle. "You boys takin' root here?" he asked.

"It's either that or sprout wings and fly across," I replied, shaking his hand as he dismounted. "Did you bring any Indians with you this time?"

He laughed at that. "Nope, but if you're lonely for some, I reckon I could find you a few."

"Never mind! That first batch you brought in was enough to last us for quite a while."

We invited Jim to camp with us, and he agreed. That evening around the campfire we heard more wild tales about mountain men and their impossible deeds. Some of them might even have been true!

The next morning we could see that the river was going down, so we knew it would only be another day or so until we could continue. Cage was teaching the boys--Britt, Moses, Davido and Eduardo--how to throw a knife, when Henry said, "Riders comin' from the north, boss."

I looked that way, and when I saw several riders heading our way, that old warning feeling began to creep up my backbone. "Okay, Henry, load your shotgun and stay by the cook wagon." I called to the four boys, "You boys get over around the bed wagon and stay under cover. Take you guns out, but be careful. Hutch, get someone to put a line on the horses to hold them, and the rest of you stay loose, but don't bunch up. I'll do the talking." Jim Cage had already faded back behind a large oak tree on the riverbank. I could see the tip of his Hawken rifle peeking around the trunk.

The riders came on, and I waited until they were fifty yards away and called out, "That's far enough! State your business and intentions."

When they stopped and the dust settled, I could see that there were eleven men in the group, and I recognized none of them. "Well, now, that's not real friendly, is it?" A sallow-faced man said. He had the look of a gambler, though dressed in range clothes. He sat with his right hand held across the saddle, kind of out of sight, and I figured he had a gun in it.

"Don't intend it to be," I replied. "We had some trouble coming up this trail from another bunch that smelled like you do, so we're not taking any chances."

The talker, evidently their leader, swelled right up. "You sayin' we stink? No wonder Hawkins wanted us to settle your hash!"

"You stink like a bunch of polecats. Now, I asked before, what are your intentions?" I had my eye on the leader, figuring I could take him and maybe the one on his right.

The man in front, the gambler, suddenly lifted his right hand, and it blossomed as he fired at me. My gun was out and shooting as soon as I saw his movement, and he missed, but I didn't.

I swung my gun right, but that man was already down, and while I looked for another target, I heard the boom and crack of Cage's fifty caliber Hawken above the rattle and bang of smaller caliber guns.

The horses the men attacking us were on were pitching and trying get away from the bullets flying around them, and the riders were at a disadvantage for all of us were on the ground. Finally, I saw three men get their horses under control and spur to the north away from the melee. The rest were on the ground, several not moving.

"Anybody hit?" I called out, meaning only the L Bar men.

They all came out from behind cover and answered up. Not one of us had a scratch, and when we began to check on the men that had attacked us, we could see that our fire had been deadly.

Of the nine men on the ground, seven were dead. The other two were seriously wounded--one in the chest, a bubbling wound that looked like a lung shot--and the other in the right side. The lung shot was unconscious, and I doubted if he'd last long. The other one was conscious, and moaning, but he looked hard hit. I knelt beside him and asked, "Who sicced you onto us?"

"That saloon keeper, Hawkins," he gasped through his pain.

"He was in jail when we left town, did the marshal let him go?"

"No, not as far as I know. Wallace, the man you shot first, worked for him as a card sharp, and he went to visit. When he came back, he gathered us all up and we followed you."

"How much did he pay you?"

"Got twenty to come, another twenty when we got back."

"Hard way to earn that little, mister," I replied.

"Wallace said it would be easy, that you were a bunch of hayseeds, and we'd knock you over like shooting fish in a barrel." He paused and drew a shaky breath. "Some fish. Some barrel," he gasped as his eyes rolled up, and he was dead.

"The other one has pegged out too, boss," Hutch said.

I stood and looked at the carnage. "Well, they don't deserve it, but let's dig some graves and bury them."

We did that, and since we didn't really want to camp next to the graves, we moved our plunder on down river a half mile or so.

The next day the water had gone down enough to cross, so we headed on south. Jim Cage rode with us, and I suggested to him that if he wanted to trail on to the L Bar, he'd be most welcome. He grinned at me, and didn't reply for a bit, and then, "You know, Earl, I don't really know how old I am. Left home when I was a sprout, and the years have just sort of rolled along, and they've been good years. I saw the Shining Mountains when they were fresh, and not a white man to be seen other than us trappers. Lived with and fought Injuns all over the place, and sure enough liked the freedom. Now, though, all my old friends are dead or gone, and I reckon my time will come one of these days, too.

"Don't feel it most days, but I must be gettin' some old too. Cold mornin's bother me more than they used too, and I find that I've got a cravin' for salt. Maybe settling down wouldn't hurt, as long as I feel like I can go when I want to."

It was the longest speech I'd heard from Jim, so it must have been on his mind for a while. "Well, you'd sure be welcome at our ranch. And, if you don't want to bunk with the cowboys, we can always build you a cabin of your own."

He was quiet again for a while, and I waited. Finally, he asked, "How do you think your wife would take it, you haulin' back an old smelly trapper to live on the place?"

I laughed at that. "I don't know how you normally smell, Jim, but right now I don't think you're much worse in that department than the rest of us. I figure to take a bath just before we reach home, but if that's not on your mind, I don't think Glory will have many objections. Just stay downwind of her."

He chuckled and we rode on.

When we got to the North Canadian, we found it on the rise, but we were able to swim the horses on over, and we camped that night on the south bank. There was a herd of cattle bedded down on the south side, evidently waiting for the water to go down before crossing. Seemed kind of strange considering that the river could have been crossed without much trouble earlier in the day.

Hutch and I rode to the cattle camp to say "Howdy," but we were not met with the usual good-natured greeting. Instead, a large man wearing a floppy black hat and a very dirty shirt, and with brown tobacco stains in his blond beard, stood from the campfire and said, "What do you want?"

I remembered that I'd greeted the men from Abilene that tried to kill us with nearly the same words. Looked like this man felt threatened, too. "My name's Earl Lamar, of the L Bar down in Bosque County. Just delivered a herd to Abilene, and thought you might like to know about trail conditions."

He didn't ask us to get down, nor did he seem all that interested in hearing about the trail. After a silence, he spat a brown steam of juice to the side and replied, "I reckon we'll find out about the trail for ourselves."

Hutch pulled in a noisy breath, probably expecting me to take offense, but there was something strange about this whole thing, and looking around I saw that these men were not really cowboys. None of them had a Texas look, and all were heavily armed and slovenly. "Suit yourself," I said, and turned my horse around to go back, though casting backward glances until we were out of gun range.

"What do you think, Hutch?"

"Well, they're not regular drovers, and did you notice the single cinch on the saddles? Those men are not from our part of the country. Maybe they didn't come by that herd honestly."

"I'm thinkin' the same thing. Let's post a guard tonight, but not move out real early tomorrow. I'd like to see how that bunch handles cattle in the morning. By the way, those are Texas cattle, and I saw a Slash S on two of them, but that brand didn't show on any of the horses. Seems like I've heard of the Slash S somewhere south of us."

"Yep, that mark belongs to Old Harold Simms, has a place down in the Hill Country around San Saba. I met his foreman in Fort Worth when I was looking for hands. He said they were putting a herd to together to trial north, and he was looking for hands, too."

We kept watch that night, and I took the last one, but all was quiet. Henry took his time fixing breakfast, and the sun was high when we sat around the fire and ate. In the mean time we saw a few men on horseback go out to the herd and come back in, but no move was made to line them out. The cattle were scattering a bit, something no drover would allow, unless he was grazing them, and it looked like the men didn't really know how to gather them in.

Hutch and I went down to the river to take a look at it while the boys and Henry packed the wagons. The water was no higher than it had been when we crossed the day before, and there were places where the herd could cross, but no effort was being made to do that. In fact, we never saw anyone even go to check on the water.

We lined out and headed on south, but Hutch and I agreed that we'd keep our eyes open for Texas men looking for a stolen herd. The main Canadian River was down enough that we crossed without any problem, and we were almost to the Washita River when we saw a group of men headed our way. Hutch recognized the man in the lead as Alvis Weatherly, the foreman for the Slash S.

"Howdy, Hutch," the man said. "Seen a herd of longhorns with a scruffy lookin' bunch of Yankees pushing them north?"

Hutch stuck out his hand to shake. "Sure did, about two days ago just this side of the North Canadian. They looked kind of suspicious to us."

Weatherly was big man, and he visibly swelled when he heard Hutch's words. "I reckon that's the bunch. Did you see any brands?"

"Slash S on the left side, and an under slope earmark on the right ear."

"Yep, them's our cattle. Ran on us this side of the Red, and before we could get them stopped, a bunch of low life swept down on us. Killed two of my men, and hied off with the cattle. We buried the boys, and we've been on their trail since."

Hutch beckoned to me, "This is my boss, Earl Lamar of the L Bar in Bosque County, Alvis."

The black haired man shook my hand, and said, "Pleased to meet you, Mr. Lamar. My boss, Mr. Simms, ain't with us. He trusted me to take the herd to Abilene and sell it, so I've got to get them back. How many was in that bunch of jayhawkers?"

"I counted ten around the fire, and maybe two or three more were out with the herd."

"Uh-huh, well I've got these eight. Two wranglers and the cook are followin' us, but I reckon we better keep on going to catch up with thieves."

"Willing to listen to a suggestion, Weatherly?" I asked.

"Shore, as long as it don't take too long."

"It won't. Here's my suggestion: my men and I will go with you, and our wagons and boys will keep on south until they come up with yours. My cook will tell your boys what's happening, and then both groups can follow us back north." As bad as I wanted to get home, I knew that if the roles were reversed Weatherly would have been quick to help us.

"Sounds good, Lamar, and I appreciate your help."

Quickly I told the crew what was happening, and with some provisions from Henry in our saddlebags, and bedrolls behind our cantles, we headed north at a trot.

Though there were heavy clouds in the west, the rain held off for the next two days and we steadily gained on the rustlers, and finally found them between the North Canadian and the Cimarron.

It was a clear evening when we began to come up to them. We had intended to camp earlier, but didn't find a spot to suit us. Now we were approaching a small creek that emptied into the river to bed down, when we heard the lowing of cattle and smelled their close presence.

As we sat our horses, Alvis said, "Looks like they're just over that low ridge, Mr. Lamar. How do you want to handle it?"

I was a bit startled at this since it was really a Slash S show, but I replied, "Let's pull back a ways and camp for tonight. Before the light goes, I think we can sneak up to the top of the ridge and get the lay of the land. Then, just at daybreak we'll head out in a surround, taking the rustlers as we come to them."

"Sounds good, so let's do it."

Three of us--myself, Jim Cage and Alvis--left our spurs on our bedrolls, and crept up the side of the ridge that separated us from the rustled herd. As we neared the top we removed our hats and slowly raised our heads high enough to see over. The light was going, but we could easily make out the herd bedded down on a flat just this side of the river. There were two men on horseback riding around the cattle, and more clustered around a campfire near the wagon.

By unspoken agreement, we all three slid back down the slope and came to our feet, not speaking until we were back in camp.

"Looks like a surround first thing tomorrow will work, Mr. Lamar," Alvis said.

"I think it will. Let's get all the sleep we can, and be saddled and ready just before daylight."

The next morning as light was just beginning to spread east across the land, fourteen of us crested the ridge and headed for the herd. We didn't run our horses, not wanting to spook the cattle, and we divided to go around both sides. As Jim and I came to the first rider, he saw us and whirled his horse to get away, but Cage, casually pointed his Hawken and it spat fire. The man threw his arms up and slid off his horse.

Cattle were coming to their feet all around now, but not looking too worried, even though they could hear gunfire. Jim and I separated, he went on north, and I turned back south, trotting my horse. As I rounded the southern tip of the herd, I saw a rustler headed my way at a dead run. I yelled, "Hold hard!" but he ignored my order and veered away to the right, firing a revolver at me as he turned.

I was riding Crowbait, the steadiest horse I owned, and one that would stand under gunfire, so I whipped my Henry rifle to my shoulder and fired when the sights filled with the gunman. His shot had missed, but mine didn't, and he plunged off his running horse.

The man was moaning when I stopped my horse next to him. I could see that my aim had been off a bit, for he was clutching the right side of his chest. A lung shot from the looks of the foam around his mouth. I wasn't too worried about him getting up and running off, so I dismounted and picked up his gun, then climbed back into the saddle, turned Crowbait and looked for other rustlers.

Trotting toward the fire, I saw that Alvis' men and mine had the rest of them down on the ground, some still alive. I joined them as Jim Cage came riding in from the north. "Did you get them all?" I asked.

"Looks like it, Earl," Hutch replied. "Angel here," he motioned to our rider in the large black sombrero, "shot their leader, and I downed one and that took the starch out of the rest of them, along with a few well placed bullets. How'd you and Cage do?"

Jim said, "I left two dead over on the other side of the herd."

They all looked at me, and I said, "There's one lying on the south side with my bullet in his chest. He looked alive when I left him." The men nodded. "Any of our men hurt?"

"Couple of scratches is all. We were lucky. Taking them by surprise they didn't have time to get organized. Plus, they were a lazy lot, no guards except the men out with the cattle."

There were six of the rustlers still alive, two of them wounded. When I rode back to see the man I'd shot, he had expired. I hoisted him up on his horse's back and went back to the fire. The men had heated up coffee on the rustler's fire, and were hunkered down sipping out of their own cups. "Boss, what should we do with these six that are still breathing?" Hutch asked.

"That's up to Alvis," I replied. "It's his herd and they're his prisoners."

Weatherly lowered his head as he thought for a minute. "Well, it's still a long ways to Abilene, and I don't have men enough to guard them and drive cattle, too. I reckon the best thing to do would be to hang 'em to a tall tree down by the river. What do you think, Mr. Lamar?"

I slowly shook my head. It was a grave decision. "Alvis, I understand your reasoning, but hangings can do some really bad things to the men that do the hanging. Personally, I don't want to take part in that. Now, we had some trouble with the men in Abilene that took exception to one of my wranglers, a boy that happens to have a black skin, and from what I heard, nobody in that town likes Texans much, regardless of their skin color. However, they have a marshal named Smith that was fair with us, and if you decide to take these men in, I'm sure he'll do his best for you."

"You think we should take them in?"

"I do. Did you ever see a hanging, Alvis?"

"No, sir, I haven't."

"Well, I did in the late war, and while I didn't have anything to do with hanging the men, my outfit came by just after they were hung, and it sure upset a bunch of us. We'd seen a lot of dead men by that time, but somehow a man dead from a bullet was one thing, one with his neck stretched was something else.

"The hanged men had been renegades, bushwhackers from both sides, and from the signs on the bodies we could see that they'd been hung by a troop of Yankee cavalry for raping and murdering civilians. We were chasing the Yankees, though we never caught up with them, but if it had been our side we would probably have done the same thing. There's no doubt the bushwhackers deserved what they got, but the image of those men dangling by ropes from tree limbs sure enough has stayed with me."

"I think I get your drift. Okay, we'll take 'em into Abilene along with the cows. I reckon we can teach them to herd cows and do other chores. Thanks for all your help, Mr. Lamar." He held out his hand and I shook it.

"No problem. If you don't need us for anything else, I think we'll head off south and find our wagons."

We parted company there and headed back south.

We met the wagons just on the other side of the Canadian, and since the river was down, we helped Weatherly's men take their wagons and the cavvy across, and then turned our wagons back south again. The boys had been very disappointed when I'd told them to stay with the wagons, and now they wanted to hear all about how we helped Alvis get his herd back. I left that up to Jim Cage, and he spun a big windy about a ghost rider and a lightning storm that had all of us laughing, and the boys didn't know what to believe.

It was early August and the weather was hot; in the next two days it got hotter. I decided that we and the livestock would do better if we traveled early in the morning, and late in the evening, finding some shade to lie up in during the hottest part of the day. I was still anxious to get home, but punishing ourselves and our animals would not get us there any faster.

We came up to the Washita River late in the afternoon, and went on across and then traveled on until the light went completely before stopping for the night. The next river we would come to would be the Red, and that meant we were getting pretty close to home.

The next morning I once again found myself urging my horse to a faster gait, and Jim Cage laughed at me. "Can't wait to get home to the little woman, huh?"

I laughed at myself. "Right you are. She was supposed to have a baby in June, and I'm real anxious to make sure both of them came through that okay. Plus, I've got a little boy a year old that I sure do miss." I looked over at him. "You ever have a family, Jim?"

He got a far away look in his eye, and replied, "Did once when I was young. Teal Wing was Shoshone, and as pretty as could be. We married according to her tribal rites, and we were also hitched up by a Catholic priest that traveled through the Idaho country. Like you, I had a little boy, too. Well, I went off trapping one winter, gone for over a week, and when I got back a raiding party of Blackfoot Indians had hit our village. Killed a lot of folks, including Teal Wing and little Red Hoss. Never tried marriage again." His voice tailed off, and I could see that though it had happened a lot of years ago, he still carried the grief with him, so I let the silence grow.

Finally, Cage slapped his leg and cackled. "Haven't thought about old Lige Mathews in years. He wintered with me and the Shoshone one winter, and nearly got his hair lifted by one of our own braves. Lige liked a young woman that was the chief's daughter. She was really too young to wed, but Lige took to hanging around her. Well, she had another suitor, a young brave with two scalps tied to his horse's mane, and he let Lige know that he didn't like him hangin' around the girl.

"Now the girl, like all females, was some flattered at the attention of these two men, and she wasn't above playin' them off against each other. One day she'd evidently asked both of them to come see her after dark, for when Lige crept up to the teepee and was about to scratch on the side to let her know he was there, the brave came up off the ground with a knife in his hand.

"It was a full moon night, and the cries and commotion roused the whole camp. Old Lige out with his blade and the two of them were circlin' each other when the chief came out of his lodge followed by the girl. He called a halt to the fight, and being a wise man and seeing that this girl was trouble, he pulled her out in front of him and made her choose. After a little hesitation, she went to the brave and touched him on the arm.

"Next day the brave brought two ponies over to the chief's teepee for a bride price, and he and the girl began building their own teepee."

"What happened to Lige?" I asked when it seemed the story was over.

Again Jim cackled. "Well, he was some put out, but at the wedding feast he recovered enough to spot a likely looking widow, the chief's sister. She gave him the eye, and she didn't have a brave of her own, so a week after the brave and the girl were married, there was another wedding, Old Lige and the widow tied the knot."

We rode on until late morning when the heat was building fast, and then stopped in a copse of oak trees near a small stream of water. Once the animals were taken care of, we all bedded down to sleep through the heat of the day, though as hot as it was, and as much as we were sweating even in the deep shade, most of us had a hard time drifting off.

Once the sun was down, we headed out again, and we were not far from the Red River when we finally stopped. The next morning I was up way before dawn. The wind was in the south, and I was sure that I could smell the Red, though it was probably just my imagination.

Henry fixed breakfast, and as soon as we could we were mounted up and on our way. It was mid-morning when we reached the Red River, and we could tell that it was rising. When the Red was down, there were sand bars showing all along its length, but when the river rose, those bars disappeared. As we sat on the north bank and looked over, there were no sandbars in sight.

"What do you think, Earl?" Hutch asked.

"Looks like she's on the rise," I replied. "Still, it's not too high yet. I think I'll give it a try."

Jim Cage spoke up: "Let me, Lamar. I've crossed more rivers than you have, and my clothes aren't near as pretty." We laughed at that, since all of us were wearing rough-looking clothes, and Cage kicked his horse and slid down the bank. We watched as he urged his mount on out into the moving water, and while he had to swim a bit right out in the middle, for the most part the water was no higher than the horse's belly.

With ropes and outriders we soon had the wagons across, and before long we were all on the other side. It was getting hot, and there was a nice grove of hackberry's and willows on the south side of the river, so we decided to hole up there until evening.

In the afternoon thunder began to rumble, and we could see lightning streaks off in the southwest. Henry was cooking an early supper so that we could eat before we took out, and the rest of us went out to the edge of the trees to look at the storm building. Great dark clouds with a greenish tinge were roiling and building, and they seemed to be headed right for us. "Think there's a twister in that cloud, Jim?" I asked.

"Yep, sure looks like it. Saw one up on the headwaters of the Cimarron a week before I hitched up with y'all, and it shore tore up the country."

I watched the cloud for a few minutes. "Wouldn't be a good idea to get caught out in the open if a twister drops in. Hutch, how about taking a look along the south bank of the river and see if we can shelter our horses and Jefe there?"

"Will do, Earl." He went off to check the river bank out, and I continued, "Henry, let's eat up and stow everything away. Maybe we can get the wagons under the bank too. If not, we'll just have to tie everything down and hope it'll still be here when the storm passes. You boys get a rope on Jefe and each of the horses so we can lead them to shelter."

For the next half hour we were busy as bees. When Hutch came back he reported that there was a long shelf down river mostly out of the water and with a high bank on the south that should hold the wagons, the horses and the rest of us, and Henry hitched up the horses and followed him down.

The Red River hadn't risen much since we crossed, but I figured with the storm that was coming that could change in a hurry. The shelf Hutch had found was along the high south bank would shelter us from the wind, unless it came right over, but we'd have to keep an eye on the river. The last thing we needed was to get caught in a flash flood.

We all knew how strong tornado winds were, and if the one coming decided to drop down on the river, we would be in real trouble. With the power of a twister, we could all be picked up and scattered to who knew where.

By the time the rain started in front of the storm we were as secure as we could be. I was standing with Cage on the bank watching the cloud move our way, wearing a slicker. The old mountain man had been in so many storms he didn't try to keep from getting wet. "A little water never hurt anybody," he said. "Why, you never can tell, it might even make me smell better!"

The wind picked up and started to blow hard, and we slid back down the bank and hunkered down with the rest. The horses and Jefe were some excited, but the boys were standing among them, talking to them, and that seemed to comfort the animals somewhat.

Now the sound of the approaching twister was a constant roar. I crawled up the bank and looked over. I could see a funnel dropping down out of the twisting black and green cloud, and it looked like it was headed off to the south of us, but I knew that could change in a heartbeat.

Back in the shelter of the bank, I waited with the rest and in a few minutes the noise dropped somewhat, and then seemed to move off. There was still a lot of rain, however, and the thunder and lightning was constant.

It was another thirty minutes before the storm moved away enough that we felt safe about moving off the shelf and back up to the prairie, and it was time to go. The Red River was rising rapidly, and we had to help the wagons up over the bank with ropes tied to the frames. Finally, we were out and could see the path of the tornado. There was a half-mile wide strip of destruction, with uprooted trees and brush, and dead animals that had been swept up in the funnel cloud.

The sky was overcast and the air was cool behind the storm, and we decided to travel until it got hot. Soon we were well away from the Red River, traveling toward home once again.

From the Red River we made it back to the L Bar in record time--yes, because I pushed the rest of them and the animals, and the others all laughed at me, but they kept up, too. It was a lovely Tuesday morning, and I was riding Sunny when I saw the buildings ahead, and with little prompting from me, she broke from a trot to a lope, and finally a headlong run. Gloria must have heard the hoofbeats, because she was coming down the steps from the front porch as I pulled Sunny to stop and made a flying dismount.

We finally released our hug enough to climb the steps to the porch, and then on into the house. "Come and see your new daughter," Glory said, and I looked at the tiny sleeping girl in the crib. Little Ralph came toddling in from the kitchen with Rachel right behind him, and I dropped to my knees to gather him in a great hug. He was laughing and crying out, "Da!" and I guess I was crying too, though silently.

I sat down on the couch with Gloria on one side and Ralph snuggled up against the other. Rachel placed the sleeping baby in my lap, and then leaned down and kissed my cheek. "Welcome home, Mister Earl," she said with a smile, and I beamed at her. Knowing we wanted to be alone, she quietly went back to the kitchen to give the Lamars time to get reacquainted.

"What did you name the baby?" I asked Gloria.

"Eleanor Flora after our mothers, just as we planned if it was a girl. I call her 'Ellie'."

I looked down at the sleeping little girl, as lovely as her mother. "She's almost as pretty as you are, babe."

"Ha! You haven't seen me in so long, you'd say I was pretty if I looked like a fencepost."

I laughed at that. "Maybe, but you'd be the prettiest post in the fence."

After while we stirred from the couch and went to see the rest of the family. Both Juanita and Rachel were now near their time for delivery, and Jimbo and Pablo were very attentive to them. Our family was growing almost by the day.

It was late afternoon when I finally went out to see about my horse, but I found that the men had taken care of her without disturbing me. After supper, Gloria and I with our two children went out to sit on the front porch, and the hands came to stand around and sit nearby. They had made some little gifts for the new arrival--whittled out dolls heads, whistles and flutes from willow branches. Bill had a carved piece of old ivory made into a pendant with a finely braided buckskin chain that would go around Ellie's neck when she got older, and Jim Cage had an Indian headdress he'd picked up somewhere, one for Ellie and one for Ralph, plus he promised the other two boys he'd make them each one.

Of course the standard comments were made about the baby girl being lucky that she took after her pretty mama in looks rather than her not-so-good-looking father, and they received no argument from me.

Little Ralph was playing with Ramon and David, but he would occasionally leave them to come over and touch me, or want a hug. It was an altogether great homecoming for me, and even the older cowboys seemed pleased that we were all back home in one piece.

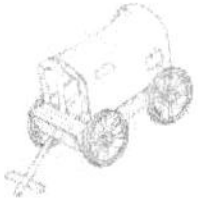

The next morning, after perhaps the most restorative sleep I'd had since I was last in our double bed, I rolled out early, leaving a sleeping Gloria looking like an angel. I silently went to the children's room, gently touching both of them, maybe to make sure they were really there. I thought how much I wished Ma and Pa were still alive and could see their grandchildren.

The men left behind had given me a good report of how things had gone, and we'd had enough rain to keep the pastures going. Pablo and Jimbo had cut hay twice, and the barn loft was full, plus they had fenced in a large stack on the other side of the horse pens.

I went out in the early quiet morning and walked around the buildings, looking things over, and while I was in front of the barn, Bill and Red came out of the bunkhouse to join me. "Checking up on us, huh Earl?" Red asked.

"You bet I am. You've probably been sleeping until noon and letting Pablo and Jimbo do all the work."

They both laughed, and Bill responded, "You don't know that little wife of yours as well as you think you do. Every Saturday she had the four of us come to the house and give her a report on how things were goin', and she wrote our comments down in one of your books."

I was pleasantly amazed. "Did she really? Why, I never asked her to do that."

"Maybe not, but she did it all the same. Kind of tickled us at first, and then we saw that she was taking up where Mrs. Lamar left off. You know, when your pa went on a cattle gather, your ma always had the hands report to her."

"I'd forgotten that, but she did, didn't she? I remember one of those times when Pa took Hutch and went down to Waco to for some reason, I must have been about ten, and she included me in the group. I hadn't been cleaning the horse corral like I was supposed to, and she sure enough got all over me about it."

"Uh-huh, I remember that," Bill said. "Red and I were told to make sure you did your chores, and we shore had fun keepin' your nose to the grindstone."

Those were good memories, even though I'd felt Ma or Pa's switch on my backside more than once for shirking the work laid out for me.

When I went back to the house, Gloria was up feeding Ellie in the kitchen, while Ralph sat in a high chair eating--or at least attempting to eat--some mashed potatoes with a spoon. When he saw me, he immediately threw the spoon away and held up his arms to be picked up. I kissed Gloria and the baby, and reached for Ralph. "He'll smear your shirt, dear," Glory said.

I threw Ralph into the air and caught him, much to his delight. "Not the worst thing that ever happened to me," I replied.

Once I had put him back in the high chair and recovered his spoon, I sat and watched my family. "Red and Bill told me that while I was gone you called them on the carpet once a week for an accounting."

Gloria blushed. "Oh, I hope they didn't think I was calling them on the carpet, Earl! You didn't tell me to, but I just thought with you gone I should know what was happening, so I asked them to give me a report, but I was real sweet about it."

I kissed her, and replied, "They didn't say you 'called them on the carpet', that's just my little joke. As a matter of fact they respected you for it and reminded me that my mother had done the same thing when Pa was gone. And, I appreciate it, babe. I want you to know everything about the ranch, and since you've started asking for reports, I'm going to involve you more in the business end of things, and have you present if possible whenever Hutch or the other men report happenings to me."

"Oh, I don't want to have the men think I'm some pushy woman with her nose in everything...they won't, will they? It's just that this is our home, and I know how the ranch must support us and all the others living here, so I want be interested in it. Does that make sense?"

"Absolutely, and the men are not going to think you're pushy. Hutch, Red and Bill all know that my mother knew everything there was to know about raising cattle and what happened on the L Bar, and they'll quickly inform the other hands."

"Good. I couldn't follow in better footsteps, even though I never had the honor of meeting your parents."

"I've been thinking how sad it is that Ma and Pa passed before they got to know you or see their grandchildren. Still, you may think I'm a little touched by the sun or something, but I feel like they're kind of lookin' down on us and smiling."

She had tears in her eyes when she looked up at me. "I'm sure you're right, Earl. Sometimes when I'm working around here and all by myself, I feel like there's a presence in the room with me, a happy, smiling presence. Think that could be your ma?"

"Oh, yes. Ma was always happy, and she sang most of the time. In one way I'm glad I wasn't here when she got so sick and kind of wasted away. Since I never saw her that way, I'll always have a picture of her in my mind as the happy, laughing woman I loved when I was home." We were both quiet for a minute, and the presence Gloria had spoken of seemed to be hovering right over us.

"Now, on another subject, do you want to go to town with me today? I have a large money draft that will have to go to Fort Worth to be banked, but I also have some cash money I want to put in your dad's safe. We can take the babies and anyone else that wants to go."

She thought about this for a minute as the baby stopped nursing and fell asleep. "Yes, I'd like to go. Red took me in once after Ellie was born, but I haven't been since. Of course, Mom was here for a week before I delivered, and a couple of days after, and Dad came out several times, the last time just after Ellie was born, so I'm sure they'd like to see their grandchildren."

"Good. This is Wednesday, but I'll pay all the hands today and some will probably want to go in with us. Also, I paid off the men Hutch hired for the drive, and they'll be going back to Fort Worth."

"Are you going to send the draft to the bank with them?"

"No, though not because I don't trust them. I want to take the draft in myself and establish an account there, and I know that will require my signature. However, I'm a little leery of having all our money in a bank, and I think I'll bring some of the money back to put in your dad's safe."

## Chapter Nineteen

Since all the hands were now flush, everybody but Hutch and Jim came along to Meridian with us. Hutch said he'd seen enough towns--and certainly that included Meridian--that he didn't need to go in for a while, and he'd stay home and keep an eye on things, and Jim said he'd stay and keep an eye on Hutch. On the trail those two had become good friends.

It was quite a cavalcade that entered the town just before noon. Gloria and I were in our buggy with the children--Moses was sitting in the back seat holding onto little Ralph. The other buggy held the other two families, and the rest were riding beside the vehicles, with Britt leading a horse for Moses.

In our part of the country women who were showing their pregnancy rarely went out in public, that didn't make much sense to me, but then I had no idea where that rule came from. But even though Rachel and Juanita were both very near the time of delivery, they both wanted their husbands to do some shopping for them, and they wanted to be close by to approve or disapprove of the choices. They wouldn't go in the stores, but they would stay in the buggy while Pablo and Jimbo shopped.

The other buggy headed on down the street as we peeled off at Wilson's store. Elmer and Flora must have been watching for us, for they were both on the porch waiting. As soon as I stopped the horses, Flora came to take the baby from Gloria, and Elmer lifted Ralph out of Moses' arms. We all laughed at these two grandparents, for they hardly gave the rest of us a glance.

Moses got down from the buggy and mounted his horse, and the three boys set off to see how quick they could get rid of their wages. All of them wanted to buy new horse gear, and they were headed first to the saddle shop a few doors down the street.

We'd invited Eduardo to stay at the ranch, but he decided to go back to Fort Worth with the other temporary hands and see his parents. I told him he was always welcome to come back, and Henry thanked him for being such a good cook's helper on the drive, and slipped him a little bonus.

After greeting the Wilsons the rest of the crew moved off on their own errands, and Glory and I went into the store.

"Glad to see you made it back in one piece, son," Elmer said.

"Me too, Grandpa. It was a long trail, but I sold the herd pretty well, and I've got some more money to put in your safe. Also, I've got a bank draft from an Abilene, Kansas bank for most of the money, and I'm going to Fort Worth to open an account in a bank there, but I'll bring back a sizeable amount of cash to deposit with you, if you don't mind."

"Not a bad idea, Earl. Things are changing in Austin, and that means they're going to change all over Texas. Union General Sheridan--the one that burnt and raped his way through the Shenandoah Valley in Virginia--is in overall charge of the military here, and he just ran Governor Throckmorton out of the state house and gave another Yankee general named Griffin the power to run the state. If we'd won the war Sheridan would have been decorating a tree for his crimes in the Valley, but there's no need to go down that road.

"Nobody knows how the whole thing will pan out, but I have a hunch it won't be good for us true Texans. You might want to leave a token amount in that Fort Worth bank and bring the rest home in gold to hide away in my safe."

"I think you've got something there, Elmer, and I'll do just that. Now, what's been happening here in Bosque County since I've been gone?"

"Not all good by any means. You remember you gave me your power of attorney in case someone tried to take your ranch again? Well, that didn't happen, but as soon as the new reconstruction law was passed in Washington, a couple of civilians came to town and set up what they call a

'Government Office', whatever that means. You remember that no account Justus Dearborn that tried to break up the dance--you know, the one you and Stan marched off to jail?"

"I do. A really smelly fella, as I recall."

"Well, I think those two scalawags that set up the office--Elvin Notting and John Westmont, both of them are Texans, but they've always been unionists--are here to make trouble. I've heard they hid out in Indian Territory during the war and never served on either side. Anyway, they've hired Dearborn as what the call their 'guard'. They've given him a deputy's badge, and he rides around lookin' important, and once they've worked over the courthouse records to discover who's land they can steal, he'll probably be their lead takeover man."

"What's Stan Baldwin got to say about that?"

"He's not real happy about it, but word came through from Austin that a lot of the elected county officials may lose their jobs if Griffin considers them 'Confederate sympathizers', and I reckon that fits Sheriff Stan to a T."

We talked a bit longer, and then Gloria called us in to dinner. Flora had out done herself with one of my favorites, a large pot roast with baked carrots and onions, and a mound of mashed potatoes with gravy on the side. She couldn't have known we were coming in, so she must have had the roast going well before.

After dinner, Elmer opened his safe and I place a leather bag in the drawer he had set aside for me. Inside the bag was a bit over one thousand dollars in greenbacks. That was what was left of the four thousand I'd received from the cattle buyer, after paying the hands and all expenses. I had also paid Sean O'Sullivan and Miss Hattie Groves ten dollars a head for their contribution to the herd before we left. I'd given them the choice of waiting until we returned and receive their share at whatever price I could get in Kansas, less expenses, or taking the ten ahead of time, and they'd both asked for advanced payment.

"All greenbacks, Earl?" Elmer asked.

"Yes, but I think I'll follow your advice and get some gold from the banker in Fort Worth. The banker's draft is for $36,240.00."

His eyebrows raised up at this unheard of amount. "When are you going to Fort Worth?"

"Probably next week. I know Gloria would probably like to go along, but with this much money if the word ever got out every thief in the country, including the scalawags and carpetbaggers, would be after me. I think I'll take a couple of the men with me instead."

Elmer closed the safe and locked it, then closed the door in the back of the pantry that hid it from view, and we went back into the kitchen.

Gloria wanted to go to the dress shop, and Flora was going with her, so Elmer and I agreed to keep the kids. Without being obvious about it I slipped Glory twenty dollars, saying, "Get yourself something nice, babe. You sure deserve it."

"I will, Earl...and how about you? You need some new clothes, so while we're gone, why don't you look over what Dad has here in the store?"

"I'll do that. I'm needing a pair of boots, too, so I figure before we leave town I'll go by Gus Walters' place and get him started on making them."

The women left to go to the dress shop, and while Elmer sat on a chair in the store, holding Ellie in his arms with Ralph playing with a little wagon at his feet, I pulled down some new trousers and shirts and stacked them on the counter. Elmer handed me the baby and went behind the counter to wrap up my stuff and make change. He had once offered me a discount, being family, but I refused. Elmer and Flora had been great to me, and I wasn't about to take advantage.

The door opened and we both looked that way. The man that came through was not one I wanted to see--Justus Dearborn, a misnomer in many ways, for I doubted if he even knew what justice was, and from the way he'd turned out, I doubted if he'd been born a "dear". I was holding Ellie in the crook of my left arm, and when I saw who came in the door, I naturally dropped my hand to Colt hanging at my side. "What do you want, Dearborn?" Elmer asked. "I've told you I don't want you in my store."

"Time's coming when you don't tell me nothin', Wilson. I got my eye on this store, and I figure I'm goin' to have it pretty soon, and you and yours is goin' to be out in the street!"

I waited on Elmer since it was his store, but when the dirty man put his hand on his gun, mine was up with the hammer cocked. Dearborn's eyes widened, and he jerked his hand away from the Colt as if the handle was hot. "Now," Elmer said, "you turn around and get out of here, and if you come again, I'm going to have you arrested for trespassing."

Without another word the scalawag turned and disappeared through the door. I let the hammer down on my gun and replaced it. The whole thing had happened so fast that neither of the children were disturbed. Ellie was dozing off in my arms, and Ralph was still playing with his toy wagon.

Elmer looked at me, and said, "Now you see what I mean about that skunk, Earl. He's digging around in the court records, and evidently he thinks he's found something."

"Is there anything he can trump up to use against you?"

"Not that I know of. I paid the taxes all during the war, even paid in gold instead of Confederate money just in case there was any argument afterward. I have the deed to the property in the safe, and since we bought with cash in 1854, I doubt he can come up with anything to legally hurt us."

"You know, Elmer, when the war ended, I was sure enough glad. Oh, I didn't like the way it turned out, but I was still alive, and so many of my fellow soldiers weren't. And then on my way home I met up with several useless men like Dearborn, and I realized that just because we'd fought a war didn't mean the end of mean people.

"Now, you and I only want to do our jobs and take care of our families, and most folks are like that, but if the useless men like Dearborn are going to be in charge, I reckon we're in for some more bad times."

"You could be right, Earl. It might not be a bad idea for you to stock up on staples in case food becomes scarce again."

I nodded. "Good idea. I'll send Henry in and you two can work up a list and order it. Pa built a big storage room in the house, and we can store a lot of stuff. Of course, we have quite a few mouths to feed, so we'll need a lot."

The women came back with their arms full of packages, and they had to show us what they'd found. We sat in the kitchen and looked as they laid out dress material and patterns. "I bought enough for Rachel and Juanita--they told me what they wanted--and Mom and I are going to have a dressmaking party out at the ranch next week," Gloria informed us.

I grinned at her, still holding Ellie, fast asleep. "That will work out just right, since I'm going to go to Fort Worth next week. If I plan it right, you may be all done before I get back."

Gloria's brow furrowed. "But Earl you just got home, surely you don't have to be gone again so soon."

I put my arm around her. "Glory, I have to go to the bank in Fort Worth, and I don't think I should wait on that. However, I'll only be gone at most four days, so it won't be like last time."

She didn't look too happy about it, but she knew that the trip was necessary. My wife had quickly learned that we must make as sure as possible that all of the ranch family was secure, and in these turbulent times in Texas, that wasn't always easy.

"Who will you take with you?" she asked.

"Why, I think I'll take Pablo and Jimbo. They were disappointed that they didn't get to go on the cattle drive, so maybe a trip to Fort Worth will make up for that a little bit."

"Okay, but I seem to remember a lot of excitement the last time a group of us went to that city. I certainly hope that doesn't happen again."

We had made up an outing to Fort Worth the year before including the three ranch families and Elmer and Flora. A no-good named Emeril Goethe, a crooked Carpetbag banker, had gathered a bunch of trash and kidnapped the women and children, including Gloria and little Ralph. With some danger and a lot of action, Jimbo, Pablo and I had rescued them, and turned the kidnappers over to the authorities in Fort Worth.

"We'll be very careful," I replied, grinning at her.

"Uh-huh. Just you remember that you are a husband and father now, not merely a wild Bosque County cowboy. And we don't want to lose you."

I kissed her. "Oh, I do remember that, my love. How could I forget? Every time I look at you--and the children, of course--I am reminded that I am a man well blessed by God. And by the way, have I told you how pretty you are today?"

She gave me a blinding smile, and replied, "Trying to change the subject, aren't you? Well, I'll let you get by with it this time," and she bent to give me a kiss.

Jimbo and Pablo were both excited when I asked them if they'd like to go to Fort Worth with me. They agreed immediately, and went to tell their wives. We started out the next Monday morning early, and by noon we'd made a good distance. It was about sixty miles from meridian to Fort Worth, going north and crossing the Brazos River, but the L Bar was ten miles closer, so we had about fifty to go. With our early start we figured to make it in two easy days, take care of business, and head back home.

It was mid-afternoon on Tuesday when the three of us rode into the main street of the nearest thing that passed for a city in our part of the state. Of course, by mid-1868 it seemed to have more empty buildings than full ones. The economy in Texas was poor all over, but in the large towns and cities things were much worse than in the country. We could raise most of our food, but families that had to rely on town work for a living were really hurting.

I had one friend in Fort Worth, a Yankee captain named Murphy Sorrel. He and his wife Lucy lived on the outskirts, and they had been very cordial to us when we'd brought the ladies to town after the kidnapping. In fact, Captain Sorrel had intervened with a reconstruction sheriff to make sure Goethe and his henchmen were jailed and charged with their crimes. The sheriff didn't want to arrest Goethe on the say so of Texans, but the captain had quickly convinced him that it was a good idea. In fact, the day after his refusal, the former sheriff was unemployed.

"I'm going right to the bank and take care of this check," I said. "Why don't you two come with me, and then we'll see if we can find a place to stay overnight."

"Un-huh, and how about a place to eat?" Jimbo asked.

Pablo and I both grinned at him. Jimbo was known to be able to put away large meals, though he was as thin as a rail. "I don't know, Pablo, what do you think? I'll bet we could find some hard tack at a store...shouldn't that be enough for this growing boy?"

"Si, Senor Earl, and we might even find a few tortillas to wrap the hardtack in," Pablo replied with a large grin on his face.

"Hardtack and tortillas!" Jimbo exclaimed. "Why don't you just feed me tree bark and grass? It'd taste just as good!"

We were still laughing at him when we tied our horses to the rail in front of the City National Bank. It was an imposing two-story building made of stone and lumber, and when we walked in heads turned to look at us. Evidently three riders in rough range clothes were a sight not often seen in the ornate lobby. I went over to a teller cage followed by Pablo and Jimbo. "I'd like to see the bank president," I said.

The teller looked me up and down, contempt written on his face. He was an average sized fellow with his dark hair parted in the middle and slicked down. He wore glasses pinched to his nose with a ribbon hanging off one side, and his necktie looked like it might be strangling him. "And what would you want to see our president about?" he asked in a voice with a Yankee twang to it.

I grinned at him. "I reckon that'll be between me and the president."

A smirk appeared on the teller's face; perhaps he felt safe behind the bars of his cage. "In that case, the president is not in."

Still grinning I turned and nodded at Jimbo. He pulled the large knife that he always carried out of its sheath and began to test the edge on a thumb, moving toward the teller's cage as he did so. Now, Jimbo was a very gentle man except when he was roused, but he could look as mean as a mad dog when he wanted to, and he wanted to at that moment. I looked back at the teller. "Now, let's start over. You go tell the president of the bank that there's a man out here who wants to do business with him, and see if he comes or not."

The teller's contemptuous look had turned to fear...in fact his eyes were glued to the knife in Jimbo's hands. Without a further word he left the counter and disappeared through a door. The door had no more than closed when it opened again. The man that came through ahead of the teller was fat, with a belly that pushed his vest out. He had a spreading walrus mustache under his nose, evidently to make up for the little hair on his head, and he was smiling.

"Mister Lamar," he said cordially. "I see you made it back from your cattle drive." He came out into the lobby and shook my hand.

"Yes, I did, and I want to talk business with you, Mister Hardwick, if I can get past your teller." Elton Hardwick was a Texan, and a native Fort Worther.

"Good, good." He looked with disgust at the teller, but the man had his head down over some paperwork.

Hardwick motioned to Pablo and Jimbo. "Are these two of your men?"

"Yes they are, two of my *best* men."

"Fine, while we talk business, maybe they'd like to have a cup of coffee?"

I looked at the two and both nodded. Jimbo had put his knife back in the sheath.

Hardwick looked over again at the teller, safe in his cage. "Elwood, go get these two gentlemen some coffee, and maybe a couple of those small cakes since it's too early for supper."

Elwood looked like he'd rather serve coffee to anybody else, but he dutifully answered his boss with a low voice, "Yes, sir."

I nodded at Pablo and Jimbo, and followed Hardwick back to his office carrying a set of saddlebags. He motioned me to a comfortable looking chair, and sat down nest to his desk. "Now then, Mister Lamar, how can I be of service?"

I reached into one saddlebag and pulled out the banker's draft, handing it to him. "I'd like to open an account here in your bank, and then take some cash out."

Hardwick looked at the draft, and then pulled a form out of his desk drawer. "How much do you want to put in the bank, and how much in cash?"

"Well, let's talk about the state of affairs here in Texas for a bit. My father-in-law, a storekeeper in Meridian, has been telling me about some of the things that have taken place since Governor Throckmorton was thrown out of office and a Yankee General named Griffin was put in charge by

Sheridan, that man that ruined the Shenandoah Valley in Virginia. Have you heard about that?"

"I have," he replied, "and the latest news is that a man named Davis has been appointed governor of Texas by Sheridan. He sounds like an out and out carpetbagger, so I don't think he's going to be real friendly to us real Texans."

"Okay, so what if he decides to close the banks and seize the money in them?"

"Well, there's an outside chance that could happen, but very outside. The congress in Washington wants to punish the South, but they also want our money, and closing the banks is like slaying the goose that laid the golden egg and roasting her up for Thanksgiving. If the banks are closed, no one can make deposits, nor can we loan money to the reconstruction officers."

I thought about that for a minute. "Okay, but there's still a chance, so here's what I'd like to do. That check is for $36,240.00. I'll leave ten thousand here, and take the rest in gold and greenbacks, mostly gold."

"Alright, but I should caution you; that much money will be hard to keep secret, and you may find half the outlaws in Fort Worth--and there are quite a few here--following you when you leave the city to go back home. Then, of course, if it is known that you have money, there are those who will try to take it legally or illegally after you get back to Meridian. Do you have a safe place to put the money when you get back to your ranch?"

"I do. Also, I know I'm taking a chance riding off with that much cash, but I brought along two good men who will be strong guards, so we'll take our chances. I don't suppose there's any way you can bring the cash in here without that Yankee teller of yours knowing about it, is there?"

He laughed at that. "You noticed Elwood isn't from around here, huh? Well, don't worry about him. He's my wife's cousin, a no-good cousin, I might add. He'd gotten into trouble in Chicago, so I agreed to let him come down here and work for me, but since the law is still looking for him up north for his part in a lumber yard robbery, I don't think you have much to worry about. He knows I'd send word to the authorities up north in a minute if he tried to pull something."

"Still, the man looks sneaky to me, and I'd rather he doesn't know anything about how much money I'll be carrying."

"Okay, let's do it this way. I'll lock your check away today, and tonight--say about nine o'clock--you meet me back here and we'll take care of our business. Elwood will not be here, and I won't tell him why you came in."

I nodded. "I think that might work. That way we can be on the road before sunup and even if he does try to arrange a robbery, it will be too late."

We agreed on that plan, and I left the draft and my saddlebags with him, watching as he locked them in a personal safe. Once I was back in the lobby I nodded at Pablo and Jimbo, and they left their coffee cups and followed me out the door.

"Well, Jimbo, if you're still hungry, we'll find a place to eat." He let us know that he thought he could eat a bite more, and we climbed on our horses and headed down the street.

We received some interesting looks when we entered the café and took seats around a table at the rear of the room, but no one said anything, and we were served without comment. During the meal I told the men in a low voice what the banker and I had arranged. Pablo said, "That is a good plan, Senor Earl, for while you were in the office with Mister Hardwick, a rough looking man came into the bank and talked to the teller."

"Is that right? I wonder what they talked about."

"We couldn't hear what they were saying," Jimbo picked up the story, "but they both looked real guilty of something."

After we'd eaten we went to look up Captain Sorrel at the Provost Marshal's office in the county courthouse. He was happy to see us, and insisted that we stay the night with him and Lucy, for he wanted us to see his new son. I thanked him, and then took him off to the side to explain what our evening plans were. "All the more reason to be at my place tonight," he said. "I'll come with you right now, and you'll be out of town until you keep your appointment with Hardwick."

We rode on to the outskirts of Fort Worth, not a long distance since the town wasn't all that big, but to make sure we weren't followed, we stayed out of the main streets. Lucy made us welcome, and we all made over the baby, just six weeks old. It would be a few hours before supper, so we sat down to visit. Lucy wanted to know about our newest one and how Juanita and Rachel were doing. Finally, it was time for her to feed little Murphy, Junior, and she left us.

"Murphy, what ever happened to Banker Goat and his band of cut throats?"

"They're all in Huntsville right now enjoying the hospitality of the State of Texas. But you know, Earl, with the changes coming under Governor Davis, I'm not so sure things are going to be too good for you Texans. He may just spring people like Goethe, and he has the authority to do it.

"I understand he's abolishing the Texas Rangers and establishing his own state police force, which will have authority over all other officers of the law in the state."

"Does he want to start another war here in Texas? I can't see our own hotheads standing still for that kind of thing."

"Well, being in the army I don't have much to say about what the civilians in charge do. Whatever laws they pass, I'll have to obey, though, and having fought you Texans in the late difficulty, I'm not anxious to do it again."

"Amen to that, my friend."

We visited a little more, and later ate at the Sorrel's table. I waited until a quarter of eight before I mounted Sunny and headed back into town. Hardwick had told me to come around behind the building and he'd be watching for me, so I did that. It was still a long way from dark, but I didn't see anyone around as I loose-tied the horse to a hitching post and entered the building through the door Hardwick held open. As I went through the door I thought I caught movement down the alley in the deep shadows, but maybe I was mistaken.

Once inside he led the way to his office, and we sat down as before. "Now, Mister Lamar, we can do our business in private. I believe you said you wanted to leave ten thousand in the bank, and take the rest in gold and greenbacks, is that right?"

"It is."

The banker went to his safe, opened it and took out the saddlebags. He removed the check and turned it over. "If you will sign the check here, we can take care of the paperwork."

I signed, and he brought a form out of his top desk drawer and began to fill it in. "This opens your account." He turned it to me for a signature, and I read the form. "You are opening the account with the total amount of the check?" I asked.

"Yes, and once open, then you sign this withdrawal slip." He showed it to me, writing in the amount of $26,240.00. I signed that one, and he again went to the safe and pulled out a bundle of greenbacks and a heavy bag of gold coins.

He counted out $13,120.00 in bills and handed them to me to count. Then he took gold coins--twenty-dollar Double Eagles--out of the bag and counted out 656 of them, making a total of $13,120.00. I counted those, also, and he handed me an empty bag to put them in. I bagged the coins, and put them in one side of the saddlebags, put the bills in a large envelope that Hardwick provided, and stowed the envelope in the other side, buckling the straps down.

"That makes a sizeable load, Mister Lamar, and you know at this time in Texas it's a fortune. Do you think it will be safe to travel back to Meridian with it?"

"Yes, but I've got a request." I told him what Jimbo and Pablo had said about the rough looking man talking with his teller that afternoon. "So, please delay letting your teller or anyone else know that I have the money with me as long as possible."

"I will do that, and I'll keep a closer eye on Elwood." He stood and led me to the door, holding it open. I took the gun out of my waistband and held it in my right hand, securing the saddlebag strap over my shoulder with the left.

"Take good care of the rest of my money, Mister Hardwick," I said.

"You can depend on it, Mister Lamar," he replied, closing the door behind me.

To say I was nervous was probably an understatement. I rode Sunny at a walk back to Sorrel's place. Darkness had fallen, and I had the feeling that there was a thief behind every tree with a gun in his hand. When I got to the house, I dismounted and walked up the stairs, knocking on the door.

Inside I laid the saddlebags down on a nearby chair. "Everything go okay?" Murphy asked.

"Yes, but the hair on the back of my neck keeps standing up."

He laughed and the others laughed with him. I looked at my two guards. "Men," I said, "Go get your horses saddled. We're going to leave tonight. For some reason I don't think Fort Worth is going to be real healthy for us come daylight."

Jimbo and Pablo went out to get their horses, and Lucy said she would fix us some provisions to take along. When she was in the kitchen, Murphy asked, "I can't allow you an escort of soldiers to protect you on your way, but I could take a few days off and go with you myself, if you think that would do any good."

"Thanks, Murphy, but I think the best way to go is to call as little attention to ourselves as possible. If it becomes known that we're carrying a valuable cargo, every outlaw in the state will want to stop us, so maybe by leaving tonight we can get out ahead of any rumors, and be back in Bosque County before anyone knows we're gone."

I thanked Lucy for her provisions, and told her I'd bring Gloria in when I could. "You know, you two are always welcome at the L Bar. Come and say a few days or a week with us. We have an empty cabin that would just fit, and I know the ladies would really like to see you."

They promised to think about it, and I slipped out the door. In an hour's time we were well on our way southwest, and by the time the moon was full up--and it was a Comanche moon, full and bright--we felt like it was safe to make a dark camp near a creek that ran into the Brazos River.

"Do we need to have guards out tonight, Mister Earl?" Jimbo asked.

"No, I don't think so. We'll stake the horses close by, and Sunny will let us know if any stranger comes around. She's better than a watchdog."

We rolled up in our blankets and went to sleep. I awakened just as dawn was brushing the sky, and soon we had our cold breakfast eaten and were on our way again. There was a low water crossing on the Brazos where the trail went across, but for some reason, this place didn't seem safe to me. "Let's go down river a ways and see if we can find another place to cross," I said.

"Got a funny feelin', boss?" Jimbo asked.

"I do, and I'd rather be cautious than sorry."

We moved on down through light brush until we came to a quiet stretch of water. The river broadened out there, and it looked shallow. We splashed on across, and climbed the bank on the other side. In a few minutes we were back near the main trail, and as we emerged from the brush I saw a man on horseback move out to look toward the regular crossing. I didn't recognize him, but something about the way he sat his saddle looked sneaky to me.

I looked back at Pablo and Jimbo and nodded to both sides. They moved their horses quietly into the thin brush, and I rode on out to the trail. "Lookin' for somebody?" I said casually.

I could almost hear the cartilage snap as the man turned his head around. He was fairly caught, and he knew it. "No, just wondering how the crossing is."

"Why don't you turn around and face me, and we'll talk about it."

I could see his left hand on the reins, but his right was out of sight, so I eased the Colt out of my waistband, cocked the hammer, and waited. He started to turn his horse, and when he had him broadside on to me, he whipped his right hand around holding a gun. It blossomed as he pulled the trigger, but the minute I saw his intention, I'd fired, and his shot went wild. I'd held on his chest, and I saw a puff of dust as the bullet took him on the left side. He threw his hands in the air and went over backwards off the horse.

I quickly searched the brush on the other side of the trail and saw movement there. A shot sounded behind me, and another man staggered out from the brush and fell face down in the trail. Pablo rode out into the trail behind the fallen man, and Jimbo came from the other direction. We all heard the sound of more horses and looked to see two men pushing their mounts north toward the river crossing.

"I reckon they had all they wanted, boss," Jimbo said.

We climbed down and looked at the two men on the ground. They were both dead and strangers to us. We turned their pockets out and discovered that each of them had a shiny new twenty-dollar gold piece. "Looks like they were paid by someone to waylay us. I wonder who it was?"

"How about that sneaky looking teller at the bank?" Pablo asked.

"Could be, but I don't really feel like going all the way back to Fort Worth to ask him. However it happened, the word of this money we're carrying is out, so we'll have to be extra careful. The money will be what keeps our families in food and clothing for a long time to come, and I don't want some no-good taking food out of my children's mouths...how about you two?"

They both agreed, and we headed on down the trail. I asked Jimbo to ride a couple of hundred yards in front, and Pablo to do the same in the rear. That way we'd have early warning of anyone else on the road.

By late afternoon we'd seen a few riders, and a wagon or two, but nothing really suspicious. Well before dark we pulled back off the trail beside a small stream, well protected by brush from the road. Jimbo put a small fire together, cooked some bacon, and boiled coffee, and then put the fire out. Again we trusted to Sunny for a watchdog, and she didn't disappoint us.

By the stars it was about two a.m. when I heard a horse snort and my eyes flew open. I lay there gripping a gun and waited, and there was a small noise off to my right. Sunny snorted again, and I came out of my bed and rolled behind a nearby oak tree. The moon was bright and it cast shadows on in the clearing, even under the trees.

First one man, and then another crept into sight, but I had a hunch there were more. Glancing over to where Pablo and Jimbo had bedded down, I saw rumpled blankets but no men. Good, they were both alert.

Another shadow came out of the brush on the west side of the clearing, and each of the three took up station beside our bedrolls. At a nod from the one near my bed, they all fired together. I had lined my gun up with nearest figure, and when he fired, I touched off the Colt. Gunfire laced the clearing, but the killers were at a disadvantage since they were all three standing out in the open, and we were under cover.

When my man dropped, I moved a couple yards from where I'd been and waited. The gunfire ceased, and it appeared that we were all waiting. Finally, I slipped out of my position and went to the man I'd shot. He was not moving, and I thought he was dead. I felt around until I found his gun, and then moved over behind another tree. "Jimbo and Pablo, can you see your men? I think mine's dead."

"Mine's not moving, boss," Jimbo answered.

"I can see mine, Senor Earl, and he is very still," Pablo said.

"Okay, without a fire let's saddle and ride." We rolled our beds, saddled our horses, and were soon on the road to Meridian.

It was early morning when we came into town, and rather than ride up to the front of Wilson's store, we went down the alley in back. Jimbo and Pablo stayed on their horses looking around alertly while I dismounted and carried the saddlebags into the back door without knocking.

Flora was in the kitchen, and I stopped there. "Why, Earl," she said, somewhat surprised, "Where did you spring from?" She came over and gave me a motherly hug.

"Hello, Flora," I replied. "I've just come back from Fort Worth with Jimbo and Pablo...and also a couple of full saddlebags. Is Elmer out in the store?"

"He is, and it's breakfast time. Can you stay and eat with us?" I had smelled bacon frying when I opened the door, and my stomach let me know that a meal wouldn't hurt.

"I'd like that, and I'm sure Jimbo and Pablo would, too. Can you feed all of us on short notice?"

"Of course I can. Tell the men to come on in, and go talk to Elmer. I'll fry up some eggs and make a new fresh of biscuits."

I left the saddlebags in a corner, and went out the back door. "Go ahead and put the horses up, boys, and come on in. Flora is going to feed us."

They both had huge grins as they complied, knowing that my mother-in-law was a mighty fine cook.

I went back in and down the hall to the front of the building where the store was located. Elmer was arranging cans on a shelf, and he was tickled to see me. He came over with his hand outstretched. "Earl! Good to see you made it back in one piece."

I shook his hand and replied, "Did you think there was some doubt about that?"

"In these times, there's always room for doubt. Did you take care of business like you wanted to?"

"Yes, and I've got some saddlebags for you to put away, after the boys and I leave."

"Not a problem." He looked around to make sure no one else could hear, though the store was still closed. "Things have gotten worse since you left. Sheriff Baldwin has been replaced by a carpetbagger named Sam Waters, and he's hired Justus Dearborn as his deputy. Dearborn came by the store to let me know that he would come in anytime he wanted to, and I'd better treat him right."

"And how did you react to that?"

"I pulled a gun out from under the counter and marched him right out into the street and down to the jail. The carpetbagger sheriff was there, and I told him to keep his deputy out of my store, and gave him chapter and verse on the man he'd hired. Waters didn't quite know what to do, so I left him to contemplate."

I laughed at the picture, and then grew serious. "That's good, but will this Waters cause you trouble, Elmer?"

"He could, I suppose, but I wrote down everything I know about Dearborn, and sent it off to the state capital. Davis has made a statement that he wants to hear from the people of Texas, and we'll see if he means it or not."

When Flora called that breakfast was ready, we went on back to the kitchen. As usual, Flora's food was delicious, and the four of us let her know it by eating until our belts were tight.

I had nodded to the saddlebags in the corner when I came into the room, and Elmer nodded back. It wasn't that I didn't trust Pablo and Jimbo to know where Elmer's safe was, but the fewer that knew the location, the better. That way, no word would slip out that might reach the wrong ears.

When we finished the meal, we went out to our horses and headed for the L Bar. I had kept a thousand dollars out of the money in the saddlebags, most in greenbacks, but some in gold, to take care of ranch necessities.

We pulled up in front of the house and there were three women waiting on the porch, with children playing around their feet. Gloria was first up and running down the steps where I caught her up and whirled her around. Juanita and Rachel were not far behind in getting reacquainted with their husbands, though in a more discrete way.

"You'd think I'd been gone for a month," I said, still hugging Glory.

"It seemed like it, too." She looked up at me. "Did you have any trouble getting your business taken care of?"

"Not really. Oh, some men tried to argue with us at the Brazos River crossing, but we asked them real nice to go back to Fort Worth, and they did."

She gave me her blinding smile. "Uh-huh, and there's more to that story than you're telling, too, but I'm just glad you're home so I won't ask for a full account."

Bill and Red came up to say welcome back, and they took our horses to the barn. We all went on into the house. The baby was in her cradle, and when I picked her up, she smiled at me. Little Ralph was hanging onto my leg, and I sat down on the couch with him on my lap and Ellie in my arms. Gloria sat down right next to me and snuggled up. It dawned on me that this was what life was all about, a warm home with a loving wife and fine, healthy children.

In the next days I fell right back into the ranch routine, and as the summer was very hot, we took it pretty easy. Our household was up early every morning to take advantage of the coolest part of the day. That's when the women cooked and baked, and the crew checked cattle and water sources, plus taking care of anything else that needed doing.

As soon as we got back from our trip, Pablo and Jimbo dragged more logs up from the Bosque to add to the horse pens. I wanted to upgrade our horse herd, and Pablo was excited about that. My idea was to try and buy a Morgan stud and breed some of our best mares to him. The Morgan would breed in more bone, and that would make sturdier mounts.

It was two weeks before we went in to Meridian one Sunday for church. As before, the three families rode in two buggies, and when we got to town we went our separate ways. I had asked that the others be at Wilson's store at four p.m. to head back, and they all agreed.

Of course, Flora and Elmer were excited and pleased to see their grandchildren, and if the kids brought their parents in, so much the better. Little Ralph was now walking and beginning to say almost intelligible words.

Elmer had some mail for us, one letter from the banker in Fort Worth. Before I left town the day we'd gotten back, I wrote a letter to him and one to Murphy Sorrel telling them about the two attacks on us as we traveled back to Meridian. Elton Hardwick wrote to let me know that his no-good relative Elwood had been arrested with four other men for the attempted robbery of a post office in Burleson, and he was headed for jail. This time, Hardwick planned to let him suffer the consequences of his actions.

We walked to church, arriving before the service started, which gave the ladies a chance to visit with their friends, and compare babies. It also gave us men a chance to talk about weather conditions, the price of cattle, and the new Reconstruction government in Austin.

Stan Baldwin was there, and I asked him how the new provost had fired him. "Well, Earl, he said since I was elected in 1864, the voters were obviously Confederate, and that made my election illegal. I told him that it didn't matter who had voted, I had been duly elected, and he didn't have the power to run me out. Then he showed me a notice signed by Governor Davis that stated all officials, including officers of the law, that had been elected under the Confederacy would be removed from office and replaced by loyal federal men. Well, I could see that I was out, so I packed up my stuff and move it out to the ranch."

"I'm sorry about that, Stan. You've always been a good and fair sheriff. When this recent Yankee ugliness is over, I hope you'll run again."

Just as we were all going into the church, two men dressed in city suits got down from a carriage and walked to the doors. I was standing beside Elmer and Stan as they came up, and Elmer said in a voice that was meant to carry, "Those are the two scalawags I was telling you about, Earl--Notting and Westmont." I was a little surprised at Elmer, usually a mild mannered man, and very polite.

The two men stopped with their boots on the first step, looking at first one of us and then the other. "That's right, Mister Wilson," one of them said. He turned to me, "I'm Elvin Notting, and this is John Westmont. We're not really scalawags, you know. Just two men working for the government trying to make the state of Texas a good place to live in." Notting looked hard at me. "And who might you be, sir?"

"Well, I might be anybody, but I am Earl Lamar of the L Bar out on the Bosque. I'm also Elmer Wilson's son-in-law, and we agree on most things."

Notting closed his prim looking mouth and the two climbed on up the stairs and went into the building.

The ladies came up to us then and we went on in to take our seats in the church. Pastor Wilhelm opened the service with a hymn, and I looked with pride at my young family. Little Ralph was sitting on Grandpa's lap, and Flora was holding Ellie. Glory was sitting right next to me, her hand in mine. I closed my eyes and thanked God for his blessings.

After church we talked with friends in the churchyard for a bit, and then walked on back to the Wilson's for Sunday Dinner. While the ladies were getting things ready, Elmer and I took care of the little ones. "Elmer, I was kind of surprised when you called those two men scalawags to their faces."

"Well, I probably shouldn't have, and certainly not on the church steps, and I've asked God to forgive me. But, Earl, it just kind of gets my back up to see them walking around town like they're lords of creation, when we all know they're only here to see how much money they can steal from us."

"I do understand that, and I did notice they weren't exactly welcomed in church, but is that the right way for Christians to act? Shouldn't we make everyone welcome in church?"

He thought for a minute, and then sat Ralph down on the floor to play. "Yes, Earl, I think you're right. Pastor Wilhelm's sermon this morning was all about forgiveness, wasn't it? Kind of hit me in the heart. Next Sunday I intend to apologize to those two."

"But still keep an eye on them during the week?"

"Well, I really don't know what they're doing here in Meridian, so keeping an eye on them does make sense, doesn't it?"

"Yes, it does. And also on Sam Waters, who wasn't at church this morning. Stan told me that though the man has some official title from Austin, he is beginning to call himself 'sheriff', which sounds kind of ominous to me. We both know that a sheriff is a county lawman, and that means he has legal jurisdiction over Bosque County. Of course, since Waters was never elected by the people of the county he can never actually be the sheriff, but by using the title he has placed himself over all county law enforcement. I don't like the sound of that, do you?"

Elmer sat back and began to answer when Glory called us to the table. When Ralph was in his highchair, and Ellie was placed in a rocking cradle next to Flora, we all held hands, bowed our heads, and Elmer asked the blessing: "Thank you, God, for your blessings...so many of them right here in this room. Please forgive me for my harsh words at church this morning, and help me listen more and speak less. Thank you for blessing the food and the hands that prepared it. In Jesus' name, amen."

He looked directly at me when the prayer was over, and I nodded, "Me too, Lord."

The ladies gave us strange looks, not having heard the exchange on the church steps. "Are you two keeping secrets from us?" Gloria asked.

Elmer and I laughed. "Not really," I responded. "Elmer was referring to an exchange of words on the church steps this morning, but I'll let him decide if he wants to tell you more."

"Thanks a lot, son-in-law," Elmer said. "Now, I couldn't keep quiet if I wanted to." He went on to tell Flora and Gloria about our short conversation with Notting and Westmont.

Later, when we were back home, Glory asked me if I thought her dad would get into trouble for speaking out against the carpetbaggers. "I don't know, babe. Things are changing in Texas now that the Yankees have appointed a governor. I understand that he's disbanded the Rangers and is establishing his own state police force, so I reckon things could get bad. However, your dad is a smart man, and he's got me and the crew on his side, as well as a lot of town folks. I doubt those scalawags want to take on the whole county."

I was speaking to reassure her, but in my own mind, I wasn't too sure just how things would turn out. Most folks in Texas just wanted to be left alone to pick up the pieces left from the war and try to make a living, but others saw the upheaval as a way to get rich without working for their money. It looked to me like the "get-rich-and-get-out" folks were in charge right now, and I wondered what that would mean for me and mine.

When my pa built the ranch house, he'd added many things to make Ma more comfortable--in fact, I could remember when neighbors came to call, they all wanted to see the wonders he had created for the woman he loved. One thing that amazed everyone that saw it was a bathroom with a large wooden tub that could be filled with water, and then drained out into a rock-lined hole. That room was right off our bedroom, and it was in use much of the time by the women and children in our large ranch family.

Also, Pa had diverted the creek that ran alongside the house into a cistern, and there was a small hand pump on the kitchen sink to bring water right into the house, which meant the women never had to carry water. These were all labor-saving devices, and Gloria and the others appreciated them.

However, there was one innovation that Pa had included that was unknown to anyone but Glory and myself. In the floor of our bedroom there was a secret latch that opened a small trapdoor. Under the door was a steel safe that Pa had brought all the way from San Antonio. I was probably about ten when he showed it to me, and cautioned that it was a close family secret-- only he and Ma, and now me, knew about it.

Pa told me once that he'd seen the safe on the porch of a general store, and when he asked the man who owned the store about it, the fellow said it had been ordered by a rancher who'd never come to get it. Pa offered to pay for the safe, and the storekeeper sold it to him.

Now, my pa was a smart man, and he knew that if people saw him carrying a safe around, they'd figure he had money in it, so he picked up his safe after dark one night, wrapped it in canvas and packed it in a wooden box marked, "coffee grinder". When he and Ma headed north to establish the ranch on the Bosque, the safe was in the wagon, and when they arrived at the location he'd chosen, he hid it out until the house was nearly finished. Then he made the trap door and lowered the safe into a prepared rocked up hole. Of course, when Gloria and I married, I showed her the safe and where the key was kept, and it was still a family secret.

When I got back home after my trip to Fort Worth, I'd waited until Gloria and I were alone in our room, and then opened the trap door. The key to the safe was always kept in a hollowed out bedpost; the decorative knob unscrewed and the hollow revealed only when we knew that we were totally alone. I'd placed the money in the safe, which held deeds and other ranch papers, along with more money, and a short-barreled Colt Pocket Pistol, loaded and capped.

As we were preparing for bed, Gloria was feeding Ellie and I opened the trapdoor and then the safe. "Gloria, we've got a bit over two-thousand dollars in here, mostly in greenbacks. The rest is in your daddy's safe in town. Now, if anything should ever happen to me, this is your immediate money."

"I know, Earl. You told me the same thing when you left on the drive to Kansas, so why are you telling me again?" She was nursing Ellie, preparing to put her down for the night.

I didn't answer until I closed the safe and trapdoor, and put the key back in its place. Then I sat down on the small couch next to my wife and daughter, and said, "I always want you and the children taken care of, along with the rest of the L Bar family, and even without the money in Elmer's safe, what's right here is enough to keep things going for a long while."

She got up and laid the sleeping baby down in her bed, and then came back to sit next to me, pulling my arm up so she could wrap it around her shoulders. "You're worried about something, aren't you?"

I hugged her, and replied, "A little...maybe concerned would be a better word. There's a man that worked in the bank in Fort Worth who knows about the money I took out in cash. I think he hired some men to set up a roadblock at the crossing of the Brazos River, and then tried to stop us again one night in the trail. We took care of both attacks easily enough, but I wonder how many others the man--a carpetbagger and a relative of the banker--told. I had a letter from the banker telling me that his relative was arrested for another robbery and will probably go to prison, but with the upheaval in Texas, that's no sure thing."

"Do you mean he or some of his friends might come here to the ranch and try to steal the money we have?"

"Well, probably not him, at least right now, but if the word is out that we have money, who knows how many have heard it? And just because the man himself is in jail, who knows how long he'll be out of circulation? If someone breaks him out of jail, it's possible he could come our way, I suppose, and I think he could enlist the scalawags to help him, to try and steal our money 'legally', so to speak. Even if he goes to prison, he'll get out sooner or later, and what could be better than to have his share of whatever is stolen waiting for him?"

We talked about that for a while but didn't come to any real conclusions, and after we were in bed and all snuggled up, I wondered if I was just crying wolf.

In the next days, things began to speed up at the ranch. Fall roundup would start in a couple of weeks, and we wanted everything to be ready. One morning I rode to the Snaketrack to talk to Sean Sullivan, and he told me he'd be ready. The next day I rode over to Miss Hattie Groves' Rafter G. She was glad to see me, and let me know that she and her crew would be ready, too. Both of these neighbors had added their cattle to the drives I'd made, and the money they received had helped them keep on going.

The following Sunday morning we went into town. Jimbo, Pablo and I had told the other hands about the men that tried to hold us up over by the Brazos and the next night on the trail, and I asked the married and single hands to stay on the ranch. We all felt some tension, and I didn't want to leave the place unattended, plus I didn't know what the scalawags in Meridian might be planning. Hutch had orders to bring part of the crew in if we weren't back by sundown.

I did take one hand along--Jim Cage. Jim had never been to Meridian, and no one there would connect him with the L Bar. I had a hunch he could sort of nose around and find out what was going on. Besides, Jim was a man to have along in any kind of trouble.

Jimbo, very handy with tools, had constructed three small seats that fit in the buggies for the three boys. The seats were kind of open boxes that a child could be fitted into. It had a padded seat, and rails all around, plus a leather belt to buckle around the body and hold active little boys in. We fastened the child seat to the buggy seat and put little Ralph in it, much to his delight. That put him between Gloria and me on the seat so we could keep an eye on him. She held the baby, and we were off.

Jim rode either beside or behind us as we traveled the ten miles into town, and when we got there I pulled right down the alley in back of Wilson's. "Y'all go on in with the babies," Cage said. "I'll take care of the horses."

"Thanks, Jim," I replied. "On the other side of the stable there's a small pasture. I usually let the horses loose in there."

I climbed down and helped Gloria, and then plucked Ralph out of his seat and we headed for the back door. Gloria was ahead of me, and she stepped up on the porch just as I was raising a foot take the first step. "Hold it right there, Lamar, and don't move a muscle," a rough voice said. "I got this here Henry on you, and if you move too sudden like, one of your kids might get hurt."

I stopped and looked over my shoulder. There was Justus Dearborn holding a rifle just as he said. I did notice that the hammer wasn't cocked, so at least a nervous finger couldn't touch it off. "What do you want, Dearborn?"

"Why, I've come to arrest you, Mister high-and-mighty Lamar, for vagrancy. There's a new law out now that says we can check everyone who comes to town for vagrancy, and if they don't have at least one hundred dollars on them, why they go right to jail. Then, I can go out to your ranch and relieve you of that money you brought back from Fort Worth." Obviously, Dearborn must have some connection with banker Hardwick's former teller, or at least he'd heard about the money. "If you're not a vagrant now, you will be when I get through with you." He cackled at his own wit.

I thought fast. "Well, let me put this boy down, and I'll show you that I do have one hundred dollars."

"No, sir! Just stand right there. I'm not taking any chances with you. Now, you turn and face me, and tell your missus to do the same. You'll all just walk in front of me and this rifle to the jail. There we'll see how much money you've got." I looked up at Gloria, whose face was dead white, and I nodded. She turned to face Dearborn.

Looking past the scalawag I saw Jim slip out of the stable door and begin to creep up on the man with the gun. Cage had his rifle held in front of him, and I knew his idea was to come up behind Dearborn and hit him in the head before he could cock the hammer and fire his gun. "Well, Dearborn," I said, stalling for time, "You can take me to the jail if you want, but not my family. My wife and children are going in that door."

"Now see here, Lamar! You're not giving the orders, I am..." Jim swung the rifle butt, hitting Dearborn in the back of the head, and he dropped right down on the ground, his rifle skittering away.

The door opened and Elmer came out closely followed by Flora. They had evidently been watching the scene from the kitchen window. Flora hugged Gloria and Ellie, and I stepped up on the porch and handed Ralph to Elmer. "Y'all go on in the house and stay safe," I said. "Jim and I will take care of this animal."

I kissed Glory, and helped them into the hallway, and then turned back. "What you want done with this thing, boss?" Jim asked. It was first time he'd called me "boss", and I was some surprised, and even flattered, since Jim Cage had told me he didn't like bosses.

"Let's load him in Elmer's wheelbarrow, and trundle him on down to the jail. We'll go right down Main Street, and I'll tell everyone we come to that Dearborn had his gun on my wife and kids."

Jim cackled at that. "Now, that's right smart," he said. "Let the whole town know what a bad hoss he is. I like it."

We found Elmer's wheelbarrow next to the stable. He used it to clean the horse manure out of the stalls before the Confederacy confiscated his horses in the last year of the war, and it was dry enough, but none too clean. With a little maneuvering we got the unconscious Dearborn into the barrow, and Jim picked up the handles and wheeled him out into the street. I walked out in front holding Dearborn's rifle out for everyone to see.

Since it was Sunday morning, there weren't a lot of people on the street to begin with, but I told a couple of people what had happened, and ask them to spread the word, and as we slowly wheeled the scalawag toward the jail, taking time to rest about every hundred feet, more and more people began to appear. In fact, by the time we came up to the jail, we had a real parade behind us, all murmuring. I kept on saying, "Yes, sir, this man on the wheelbarrow threatened to shoot my wife and children. This is the man the carpetbag sheriff has for a deputy, and if he has his way, none of the women or kids in the county will be safe from him."

Jim stopped the wheelbarrow in front of the jail, and I called out, "You in the jail. Come on out here and get your deputy!"

The door opened and a man in a Yankee uniform came out. "I'm Captain Sam Waters, and what have you done to this man?" he said this in a voice that he might have wanted to be rough and commanding, but there was shrill tone of fear behind it.

"This man, if you can call him that, tried to arrest me for vagrancy, he cited some new law about having to have one hundred dollars to prove I was not a vagrant. At the time, my wife and children and I were going in the back door of her parent's home. I was holding our son, and Gloria was holding our daughter. This--thing--on the barrow threatened them with a rifle. My friend here came up behind him and Dearborn stumbled against his rifle stock and knocked himself out." There were chuckles and outright laughter when I mentioned Dearborn stumbling against Jim's rifle butt.

"Well, it seems to me, Mr. Lamar, that you have broken the law by injuring a duly appointed officer of the law in performance of his duty. I can arrest you for that, as well as your man here."

My "man", as Waters called him, casually cocked his rifle and let it swing to point at the provost marshal. Waters looked kind of sick. "Is there a new law about vagrancy, mister?" I asked. I was not about to give the Yankee the curtsey of a title, "One that says everyone must show that he has at least one hundred dollars or be considered a vagrant?"

"Well, yes there is. The governor has decided that there are too many people wandering around the towns and cities of Texas with no visible means of support, and he has notified all of the peace officers of that new law."

"In other words, the carpetbag governor, appointed by a carpetbagger in Washington, has now taken over the Texas State Legislature and is making laws?" I turned to the crowd behind me. "What do you folks think of that?" There was a roar from the crowd, and Waters began nervously to finger the holstered revolver at his side.

When the crowd quieted a bit, I said, "This scum you call a deputy threatened my family with a firearm, and I am making a citizen's arrest of him for that crime. Also, I am charging you with aiding and abetting your deputy in threatening my family. Now, you're going to put him in a cell, and take down my charges and a statement of action from me and Mr. Cage. And then, I'm sending a copy of my charges and those statements to Austin and Fort Worth to be published in the newspapers. If you'd like to go ahead and arrest me, have at it, and I'll add wrongful arrest to the charges I am bringing against you and your deputy."

Waters was way out of his depth, and he knew it. The crowd behind me was growling again, and I noticed, as he did, that a few of the men were carrying ropes. "Well...uh, Mister Lamar, I guess you can to do whatever you say, but I will not jail Dearborn or take down your statements."

"Good, and I thought you'd say that, so I'm also making a citizen's arrest of you for failure to keep the peace and for inciting a riot." I pulled my gun for the first time, and motioned him inside the jail. Anything might have happened, but a voice was raised above the grumbling of the crowd, the voice of Judge Smallview. I looked over to the edge of the crowd and saw him with the two reconstruction officials, Notting and Westmont behind him.

"Earl, would you hold up a minute?" the judge asked. He was a friend, and one I had rescued from being illegally jailed by another phony carpetbag provost who had arrested him and my father-in-law some months before.

"Sure, Judge. What do you want?"

"I've heard everything you've said, and so have these two men with me. You are correct in saying that a man who threatened your family with a gun deserves punishment, but you're wrong about your ability to make a citizen's arrest. Since Governor Davis has declared martial law in this state, that law supercedes all others, and no citizen can make an arrest."

The grumbling from the crowd increased again, but the judge held up his hand, and the people quieted, for he was much respected in Meridian and Bosque County. "Now, Mr. Notting and Mr. Westmont have agreed to investigate Dearborn's actions, and they will then make recommendations to the state."

Dearborn chose this moment to begin coming back to consciousness. He snorted, and looked around, finally noting where he was, and trying to get up. In the process, he tipped the wheelbarrow over and sprawled on the ground. It was just the moment of relief the crowd needed, and a great roar of laughter went up. I grinned at Dearborn, and then said to the judge, "All right, Judge, we'll do it your way. But I think all three of these carpetbaggers should know that marshal law or not, we will not put up with having our families threatened. The next time I come to town, I better not see this piece of scum wearing a badge or pretending to be a law officer, or I'll shoot him as quick as I would a rabid dog."

Dearborn had gotten to his feet, and he started to speak, but the barrel of Jim's Hawken was suddenly under his chin. "Be careful Dearborn. You're not out of the woods yet."

The judge and the two government men came up and ushered the man on into the jail building, where Waters had already disappeared. The judge asked me and Jim to come in and make a statement, and we did. As we told what happened, Dearborn tried to interrupt, but Notting made him quiet down. When our statements were given we left the jail office and went back to Wilson's.

Everyone was waiting to find out what happened when we got back to Elmer and Flora's house. Jim was his usual silent self, so I told the story.

Church time was long past, so we ate a late lunch, hitched the horses to the buggy, and headed back to the ranch. Elmer assured me that he would keep an eye on things in town, and send out a messenger if it looked like trouble was brewing. I hoped that it wasn't, but things were very uncertain in Texas, and none of us knew what would happen with the carpetbaggers in complete control.

## Chapter Twenty-Five

When we got back to the L Bar, Gloria and I gathered everyone around, including Rachel and Juanita, and told them what had happened in town. "I don't know that anything will come of it, but I wanted you all to know. Let's be on our guard, and if any of you go to town, take someone else with you."

Hutch asked, "Do you think we'll have any trouble out here, Earl?"

"I'm not sure, Hutch, but let's not leave the women and children alone on the place. Dearborn knows about the money I brought back from Fort Worth, and we have no idea who he's told. Let's just be real careful for a while.

"When you send the men out to work, let them go in pairs, and always have at least one man around here. The fellow we had trouble with had no hesitation in threatening Gloria and the kids, and I figure a man like that will do about anything." There were no more questions, and I knew that enough was said. The men on the ranch saw themselves as part of a big family, and they would risk their lives to protect the ladies and their children.

While in Fort Worth, I'd heard reports of a secret group of hooded men that called themselves the Ku Klux Klan raiding black communities, and killing black people and their white friends. Mostly they seemed to be raiding in Louisiana and East Texas and down around Houston, but I wondered if this sinister, secret group would come to our area.

Jimbo had heard the same rumors in the black community in Meridian, and on Monday after my brush with Dearborn and his friends, he came to the office where I was plowing through some paperwork and asked if we could talk. "Sure we can, Jimbo. What's on your mind?"

"Well, Earl," he began, and I knew he was serious because he didn't call me Mister Earl, "I'm some worried about this Klan business. The last time we were in church in Meridian, a couple of the fellas told me that Dearborn was a member of that group."

"Now that's interesting. He's just the type to sneak around at night and take advantage of anyone he thinks is weaker than himself. Did your friends say there was a Klan formed in Meridian for sure?"

"No, they had just heard rumors. You know, Negroes in Meridian work mostly at serving jobs, and a lot of white folks talk around black people like they're deaf, so they hear most things that go around."

I thought about that for a bit. "Next Sunday, Jimbo, let's all go in to church. The three families will go to our different churches and see what we can find out about this gang...if there's a bunch formed or forming or not, and if possible, who is a part of it."

He smiled at that. "Sounds good, Mister Earl. I reckon we can find out a lot."

"I hope so, Jimbo. We've all faced more trouble that we want, but if we can head some kind of attack off before it starts, why so much the better.

"By the way, I appreciate the way you've taken Britt, Moses and Davido under your wing. I saw you teaching them some carpentry skills last week. How are they on reading and writing?"

"Both Britt and Moses can read and write a little bit, but they're no scholars. I'm not sure about Davido, but he may be able to read and write Spanish. Do you think we're going to have to have a school for all the boys before long?"

"I do. At dinner, let's ask the ladies how they'd feel about holding some classes after roundup. Simple things would be good for the little boys, and maybe they can include the big boys in some harder lessons."

"Uh-huh, and how will we get those big boys to go to school?"

"I have a hunch the ladies can take care of that. You and I can tell them they have to go, and they'll resent it, but I have a hunch if the ladies ask them real nice, maybe promising cookies or doughnuts, they'll agree."

Jimbo laughed at that. "Is that how your Ma got you to sit still for schoolin'?"

"No, not on your life. She used a switch, and my pa backed her up, so I didn't have much choice."

Now, he really laughed. "Me, too. You know it was against the law to teach slaves how to read and write in the old days, but my ma worked in the big house, and her mistress taught her to read and write, and Ma was bound and determined that us kids would learn, too. Well, we did. I can still feel that hickory switch on my bottom!" We both laughed at being educated with a switch, but we also knew that our parents had been right to make us learn.

Jimbo left to go out for work, and I went back to the books. In a little while, Gloria came in with two cups of coffee and sat down to visit with me. She was always as fresh as a daisy, and I never tired of looking at her pretty face. "What are you working on?" she asked.

"Payroll records," I replied. "Friday will be payday, so I'm bringing everything up to date. Thanks for keeping the books going while I was gone, babe. That really helped."

"I think the men were kind of embarrassed to take their pay from me while you were on the cattle trail. I know you always have them come in one at a time and pay them, but I didn't think that was a good idea, so I just put together envelopes for each one, wrote their names on them, and took them over to the bunkhouse, leaving them on the kitchen table there."

"That was a good idea, and I'll bet they appreciated it. How about for Jimbo and Pablo?"

"I took theirs to the bunkhouse, too. That way everyone was treated the same."

"I am married to one smart woman," I said, leaning over and giving her a kiss.

At dinner, I brought up the idea of a school beginning in the fall, and the women all liked it. Rachel came up with a good way to get the bigger boys interested--the first day of school would start with a picnic, but only for the teachers and students.

I looked at Jimbo and winked, and he hid his smile by taking a drink of coffee. Our household might have been strange to most people, but it worked smoothly for us, and we were happy about that. Rachel called us a "crazy quilt" family, because we were blessed with three racial cultures, and she was right. The crazy quilt idea had caught on, and there was no racial friction on the L Bar at all. For one thing, all were treated equally in whatever happened.

I was the overall boss since I had inherited the ranch from my parents, and Gloria was in charge of the household since she was my wife, but neither of us tried to lord it over the others. We were thankful that God had blessed us with all of them.

On Friday I paid the hands and the women, and thanked each of them for their service. As usual on payday, we had a meal together, Henry helping the ladies in the kitchen, and all the bunkhouse hands eating with the families on the tables out under the live oaks. When we were settled, and the blessing was given, I asked for suggestions about how to make the ranch a better and more profitable place for all of us.

Pablo had an idea about raising more horses, and it was a good one. Following up on my idea of improving our horse herd, a friend in Meridian had told him about a Morgan stud and four mares for sale in the Denton area. The man that owned them had died and his widow wanted to sell. "Any idea of price?" I asked.

"Only a rumor...one hundred dollars for the stud, and fifty for each mare."

"Can you find out the name of the family so we can make a contact?"

"Si, I think I can."

"Good. If you can get a name and location, you can go take a look at them."

Pablo was grinning from ear to ear. He was a good cowboy, and worked cattle without complaint, but his real love was to work with horses, and he had a sure touch with them the likes of which I'd never seen before. If we began raising our own stock, Pablo would be busy all the time. Already it was known in the area that a Pablo trained horse was the best, and if we could raise and train horses for other people, it would add to the income of the ranch.

The meal went on, and the discussion turned to the rumors about the Ku Klux Klan. Finally, in a bit of silence, Moses asked, "Boss, what if that Klan should come here to attack us?"

"Good question, Moses. My father built this ranch, and he placed the buildings the way they are to defend against Indian attacks--Comanches, for the most part. Now, some of you have fought Indians on the L Bar, so you know how we do it. For those who have not, Hutch and I will explain how we've always handled things."

I looked at Moses. "To answer your question directly, Moses, if the Klan comes to make trouble here, we'll handle them just like the Comanches...we'll fight. The L bar is not just a cattle ranch, it is our home, all of us, and if any one of us is attacked, that's an attack on all of us." I looked around the table. "Am I right?"

A chorus of affirmative answers came back. Jim Cage rarely spoke, unless he had something to say, so when he uttered a word, everybody listened. "I'm new here on the ranch, ladies and gentlemen, but I'm sure not new to fighting, whether Indians or whites. Now, I want you all to know that I sure enjoy this place, and the ladies' good cooking, and I reckon when the times comes, I'll join in."

We all laughed at that, and Henry commented, "Jim, you may favor the ladies' cooking, and I'll admit it's mighty good, but I noticed on the trail you didn't back away from my cooking all that much, nor out in the bunkhouse here on the ranch, for that matter."

Cage's eyes crinkled, and he replied, "Wal now, Henry, I reckon you're right, but you need to remember one thing: if a man's hungry enough, he'll eat just about anything, even if it's fixed by fella!"

That brought the house down, and we finished the meal on a happy note, enjoying the dried apple pies that ladies had made for desert.

On Sunday, Gloria and I went in to church with our kids, with Jimbo and Pablo as outriders. I had suggested that all three families go to church to pick up any word about the KKK, but both Rachel and Juanita were now very heavy with child, and refused to be seen by anyone but the ranch family.

It had been a week since my encounter with Dearborn, and Elmer told me that the man hadn't been seen around town, but neither had anything been done about my charges. He'd talked to Judge Smallview, and the judge told him that if anything was happening, he was not aware of it. The town was divided in a very elemental way--the original residents, and the newcomer carpetbaggers and scalawags--and there wasn't much communication between them.

If the government representatives wanted to make themselves hated outsiders, they couldn't have chosen a better way than to back a man who threatened women and children, and then fail to punish him when he was caught.

Elmer and Flora had to carry the children to church, though Ralph was getting big enough that he was quite a load. Still, that left Gloria and I with hands free, and I thought it was wise to have at least my right hand free, so I held hers with my left. At the church we visited with folks out in the front yard where there were plenty of shade trees, and I noticed that once again Elvin Notting and John Westmont were there. Elmer went up to them and apologized for his behavior two Sundays before, and they graciously accepted his apology. I stood beside him as he spoke, and then reached out to shake hands with the two men. There were no smiles, but both Elmer and I felt better about our actions.

After church, we went back to the Wilson's for fried chicken and all the trimmings. After that good meal, we took chairs and went out to sit on the back porch to let things settle. While we were sitting there enjoying a small, relatively cool breeze, Jimbo and Pablo came into the alley from the south end, and pulled up to a stop in front of the porch. Elmer invited them to get down and sit with us, and they agreed.

Since I had asked each of them to go to their respective churches and see if there was any news about the KKK, they gave us a report. "The nearest raids seem to be in Dallas County, right now," Jimbo said. "Seems like most of them are against black folks, although I did hear that a white man in Jefferson who said Negroes ought to own all the plantations, since they were responsible for building them anyway, was hung. I asked about Dearborn, but nobody's seen him for a week."

"Any stories about a Klan forming here in Bosque County?" I asked.

"Nope, but I did hear there was a small group in Fort Worth that had done some ridin' around at night wearing pillow covers over their heads tryin' to scare folks."

Pablo added, "One of my friends told me that in Waco a carpetbag official was hung a few weeks ago, but the local police caught the men that did it and put them in jail. A sign left on the body said the KKK had done it, but no one knows who it was for sure."

We talked a bit more about the clan, and then decided to head home while we still had plenty of light. It was a pleasant ride back home, though we all felt some tension about what had been discussed.

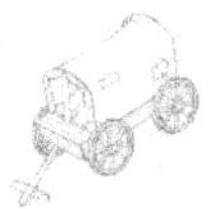

That evening, all the L Bar people gathered out on the front porch, and Jimbo and Pablo gave them the news. Finally, Hutch asked, "Earl, do we need to set a guard at night? From what I've heard these people seem to like to raid when it's dark."

"I don't know about setting a guard, Hutch, but maybe we should at least sleep a bit lighter. If anyone suspects something isn't right, come and knock on our door, and I'll come check it out. And don't worry about awakening me even though nothing comes of it. I'd rather have a false alarm than see someone hurt."

For the next several nights we were all light sleepers, but when morning came and nothing had happened, things began to go back to normal. We really had no way of knowing whether or not Dearborn was a member of the Klan, or, if so, whether he would bring some of the Klan out to attack us. It was just that we were a racially mixed group and from what we'd heard that made us possible targets. Most of the Klan stories circulating at the time confirmed that the nightriders were intent on keeping every race in its place, or at least the place the KKK had decided on.

Two weeks passed quietly, and then on a night of a full moon--a Comanche moon in our part of the country, since the Comanches liked to steal horses on nights of bright moonlight--I was awakened by a knock on the front door. I got up and went to the door, pulling a revolver out of the holster hanging high on the wall. "Who is it?"

"Jim." I opened the door and he slid through. "I think we've got company, Earl."

"What makes you think so?"

"About an hour ago, I heard the horses in the pen behind the barn move around, and one of them snorted. I eased on over there thinkin' Injuns, but I didn't see anything right off. Well, I was hunkered down by the gate when I suddenly heard two men talkin', not Injun talk, but white. One of them said, 'Where's Dearborn?' and the other one said, 'Went to those little shacks behind the house.' I went on over to the cabins, but didn't see anything, so I came and knocked on your door."

"Let me get some clothes on, Jim, and we'll make a plan," I said in a low voice.

I went back into the bedroom as quietly as possible, but Gloria was already awake. "What is it, Earl?"

"Jim says we've got uninvited company, and not Comanches. I'm going to take a look." I leaned over and kissed her. "You lie back down and don't worry. We'll sort it out."

She lay back down, and I finished dressing, picked up my guns and gun belt, and went back out, stopping only to take the spurs off my boots. Cage was holding the front door open a few inches, looking out on the moonlit ranch yard. When I joined him, he slipped out the door and moved silently off the porch into the deep shadow cast by the roof.

Circling slowly around the ranch yard, we came to the barn. Jim crouched and I followed his action. As we came to the big doors in the front, I could hear voices inside, but I couldn't make out the words. Putting my mouth next to Jim's ear, I said, "Go back to the bunkhouse and wake everyone up. Tell them to stay inside, but make sure their guns are handy."

Cage nodded and slipped away. I crept off and worked my way to Pablo and Juanita's cabin, and said in a low voice against the open window, "Pablo."

In a moment I could dimly see his face at the window. "Si, senior."

"Enemies around. Get your family up and in the house, and I'll tell Jimbo."

I ducked down and slid off to the next cabin, again speaking at the open window. Jimbo listened and agreed, and I turned and went back to the house just as Pablo, Juanita and little Ramon were entering the kitchen door.

Inside I cautioned them to not make a light and keep their voices down, and went on to our bedroom. Gloria was awake, and when I quietly told her what we'd found, she got out of bed and began to dress. "Please tell Juanita and Rachel to come in here with the boys. We'll stay in this room, and we won't come out unless you, or Pablo, or Jimbo tell us to."

"Good. I'll tell them," and I went back to the kitchen to find that Jimbo, Rachel and David were there. I sent the ladies and children off to the bedroom, and placed Jimbo in the kitchen to keep watch on the back of the house and the cabins, and sent Pablo off to the living room to look out west. I went into my office and silently opened the window, which looked out on the ranch yard.

South of the bunkhouse I saw a light, which grew as I watched. Someone had lit a fire. Then came the sound of running horses, and a group of men poured into the ranch yard--it looked like about ten of them. The one in front was carrying a lighted torch, and I saw him draw back his arm to throw it toward the porch, but a shot rang out from the bunkhouse, and the man dropped the torch and grabbed at his saddlehorn as his horse ran off.

Now shooting was all around, and I saw a man over my sights that looked like Dearborn, he was racing past the house, and I led him a bit before I pressed the trigger on the Henry. He threw his hands into the air and dropped off his horse, and suddenly there were no more riders in sight. The shooting stopped, but no one moved. Since most of us were seasoned Indian fighters, we knew that sometimes the first man to move was the next man to die.

We waited until daylight was moving across the ranch yard before we ventured out. I walked down to see the last man I'd shot at, and discovered Dearborn as dead as he'd ever be. The other men were moving around, and I went back and sat on the porch steps. Pretty soon all of them headed my way and gathered in front of me. "Four dead with this one, Earl. They all had white hoods on, and whether they were actually the KKK or just trying to look like them, I guess we'll never know. None of us recognize the other three, so they may be from out of the county."

"Okay, Hutch. After breakfast, load them in the wagon and we'll haul 'em to Meridian. You come along with me," I continued, and looking at Cage, I said, "I'd appreciate if you'd come along, too, Jim." He nodded. "The rest of you keep your eyes open around here. Since they got their fill of lead last night, I doubt if any of the riders are still around, but let's keep an eye out until we're sure."

In the house, the ladies made a quick breakfast and fed us. They were all three quiet and subdued, and Jimbo and Pablo didn't have much to say, either. When we were finished I said to the two men, "Stick around the buildings today and keep an eye on things. I'll be back as soon as possible."

Gloria followed me into the bedroom for a warm goodbye. "Earl, do you think these troubled times will ever end?"

"Yes, babe, I do. It will take a few years, but sooner or later Texas will throw the carpetbaggers and scalawags out, and we'll have peace."

"I hope so. I'd like to think that Ralph will never have to carry a gun, and Ellie won't have to load rifles for her husband to fight off Indians or outlaws."

"Me too."

## Chapter Twenty-Seven

In Meridian, I drove the wagon to the jail, and called for the provost to come out. Captain Waters came through the door, saying, "What do you want now, Lamar?"

"Making a delivery," I replied. Jim and Hutch were pulling the first of the bodies out of the wagon bed and dragging them to the porch in front of the jail.

"Here!" Waters cried out, "What is this?" he looked at the first dead man, his hood tucked into his belt.

I didn't say anything more until all four bodies were on the porch, including Dearborn. "Since one of these raiders was your deputy, I thought you might as well have him and his friends. The raided the L Bar last night. There were ten or twelve of them, but we only shot these four, and they're all yours."

He was sputtering, trying to find words, but we ignored him. Hutch and I climbed back to the wagon seat, and Jim mounted, and we turned toward Wilson's store. We were anxious to get back to the ranch, so we didn't stay there any time at all, just long enough to let them know that no one was hurt in the KKK raid.

When we went back out to the wagon, we could see that the bodies had been removed from the jail porch, but no one was around, so we headed out.

When we got back home, Gloria let me know that the ladies were working on a feed for all of us in celebration of our coming through the KKK attack unscathed. When they rang the triangle, we gathered at the outdoor tables and ate until we couldn't hold anymore.

As I sat there I looked at the group of people that made up the L Bar family, and thought how lucky I was. For one thing, I'd survived the war, and many men of my age hadn't. Then I'd had the good fortune of finding Gloria, who had brought beauty and grace into my life. Now, we had some money, and all of us were as safe as we could be in Reconstruction Texas. We had faced so many dangers--Comanches, kidnappers, scalawags and carpetbaggers--that I was confident we could endure whatever came our way.

Sitting there, I offered a silent prayer: "Oh, Lord, thank you for all of your blessings, those that have already been showered upon us, and those that are to come. Amen."

**You can find ALL our books on our website at:**
*http://www.writers-exchange.com*

**All our Historical novels:**
*http://www.writers-exchange.com/category/genres/historical/*

Intriguing tales...told Texas-style...are the hallmark of legendary children's author, Herb Marlow. The acclaimed writer, educator, and counselor offers a rich series of historic and adventure novels that are destined to become classics for children of all ages. These timeless treasures spark the imagination and remove the mystery from history as young readers interact with captivating characters and creatures.

Dr. Herb Marlow has been featured on TV, radio and in print publications nationwide. He is an established authority on childhood issues, a motivational speaker for children and adults, a professional counselor, and a rancher. He and his wife reside on a small working ranch in East Texas.

**The Writer**

Dr. Marlow has written 23 fiction books for children and young adults. In addition, he has written a trilogy of books on parenting that educate parents on issues they'll face from the time they become parents through the continuum of life, as well as several books for teachers and parents to aid them in dealing with ADD/ADHD and childhood behavioral disorders.

## The Educator

Herb Marlow is a captivating speaker and storyteller whose tales engage students and adults alike. Bringing his own real-life stories of challenge and triumph into each speaking engagement, he helps people see their worlds from a higher point of view.

In schools, children love the excitement of meeting a real author, especially a warm grandfatherly cowboy like Herb Marlow. As he speaks before each auditorium full of young faces, he finds that lives are touched and children are motivated by the stories he tells and the lessons he shares.

## The Counselor

Dr. Marlow spent a portion of his adult life as a pastor. However, seeing the myriad of heartaches faced by the people he served, he returned to university to obtain his Ph.D. in counseling and to begin a private pastoral counseling practice. He continues to provide counseling today through a unique Internet-based, on-line counseling service.

## The Man

Herb has been married to Lynn Marlow, for 43 years. Together, they have successfully raised three children.

You can keep track of his books with Writers Exchange E-Publishing on his author page: http://www.writers-exchange.com/Herb-Marlow/

**If you enjoyed this author's book, then please place a review up at the site of purchase and any social media sites you frequent!**

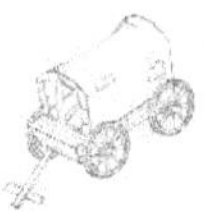

*If you want to read more about novels by this author, they are listed on the following pages...*

# Outlaws West

Sending Josh Holt and his friends home to Daddy tied backward on their horses might seem a cruel thing to do, but fast-thinking Deputy U.S. Marshal Stan Hankins figures it's better than sending them home dead.

Hankins and his partner Chico Wrath find and arrest outlaws who've fled to Indian Territory in the 1870s to escape the law. Sure-as-shooting it's a dangerous job that doesn't pay very well. Still, at the end of the day, it beats farming!

Publisher Page: http://www.writers-exchange.com/Outlaws-West/

# Winchester Battles Series

*Jonas Slaton, M.D. is a local Winchester, VA doctor when the Civil War begins. Because of its proximity to Washington D.C. and its many productive farms, the Shenandoah Valley is of vital importance to both the North and South and will be fought over many times during the conflict.*

## Book 1: Winchester Doctor

In May 1862, the Union Army under General Banks occupies Winchester but Stonewall Jackson's Valley Army remains intact, fully expected to attempt to retake the town. Preparing for the first Battle of Winchester, Dr. Jonas Slaton invites a number of people to stay in the safety of his house for the duration, including the new storekeeper's sister, Elaine, whose spell he instantly falls under...

Publisher Page: http://www.writers-exchange.com/Winchester-Doctor/

# The Laughter of God

Just who is the quiet warehouse worker named Bill Harmony?

Disturbed by the shallow sermons and self-aggrandising showmanship of his pastor, Bill confronts Doctor Littlehope privately only to be brushed off as an ignorant layman. An upcoming revival event at the church run by a TV evangelist who claims he can heal and raise people from the dead raises even more red flags. Certain this isn't the hand of God at work, Bill and his friends set about exposing the scam.

But there's more to Bill than meets the eye, and when locals begin revealing the miraculous works he's performed quietly, far from the spotlight, everyone, including his close friends, begin to ask, "Who is Bill Harmony anyway?"

Publisher Page: http://www.writers-exchange.com/The-Laughter-of-God/

# The River Series
## {Historical: Western}

*The road from Louisiana to the L Bar Ranch on the Bosque River, Texas is a long and dangerous one, but for Earl Lamar, recently discharged sergeant from the First Texas Confederate Cavalry, it's the only way home.*

## Book 1: Trouble on the Bosque

After surviving the war, discharged Confederate soldier Earl Lamar learns his parents didn't...and the responsibility of the L Bar Ranch falls to him.

After selling enough cattle to care for the original cowboys and new families, the Esperanzas and the Roses along with cook Henry Spooner, Earl has his work cut out for him keeping the ranch going with rustlers, conmen, false imprisonment and Comanche raids all presenting tough challenges to be overcome. When Earl falls in love and he and Gloria find themselves expecting their first child, he begins to hope that maybe, just maybe, a new life awaits him on the Bosque.

Publisher Page: http://www.writers-exchange.com/Trouble-on-the-Bosque/

## Book 2: Drive the Pecos

In June 1866, Texas struggles to recover from the conclusion of the War between the States. Though cattle aren't worth much in Texas, other places clamor for beef, and the Goodnight-Loving trail opens that summer to sell cattle to the U.S. government looking to feed reservation Indians. Earl Lamar, owner of the L Bar Ranch, decides to add two hundred head from his own cattle herd to Charles Goodnight's first drive to the Pecos River.

With gold in his pocket, Earl sets his sights on returning home to meet his new son Ralph, but trouble is brewing in Texas, and Meridian and Bosque County won't be left out. Rustlers, bushwhackers and carpetbaggers threaten the stability and future of Earl's ranch. A ruthless banker and his gang put Earl and his cowboys out of commission, then kidnap their women and children. Little do they realize Earl and his men are indeed alive, if not well, and have every intention of rescuing their families.

Publisher Page: http://www.writers-exchange.com/Drive-the-Pecos/

## Book 3: Red River Rising

Earl Lamar, former Confederate soldier and Bosque County Texas rancher has made two successful cattle drives, selling cattle to keep the L Bar Ranch in business. While driving his herd safely across the Red River and Indian Territory will bring in enough gold to keep his ranch afloat for a long time to come, the danger in taking the trail to Kansas can't be overlooked with treacherous rivers to cross, Indians to avoid or fight, bad weather, and ruthless cattle thieves always lying in wait.

Earl manages to return home in one piece just in time to meet his new daughter. But a carpetbagger Texas governor seems intent on playing rough with former rebelling states by making things as miserable as possible for native Texans. To make matters worse, the KKK raids Earl's ranch and Texas no longer seems to have a hope or prayer of ever returning to normal. Publisher Page: http://www.writers-exchange.com/Red-River-Rising/